THE
ALL-AMERICAN
LIEUTENANT

By

Rich Grimes

ACKNOWLEDGEMENTS AND MEMORIAM

Tom Brokaw's work, *The Greatest Generation*, celebrated the conscience and contributions of Americans who came of age during the Great Depression and fought in World War II. 16 million men and women served dutifully in that war and of that number, a mere 558,000 are still living. Sadly, we *Baby Boomers* are prone to fall short recognizing the monumental significance of their commitment to keep the world "safe for democracy," but by reading, research, and exposure to documentary evidence, much can be learned. That said, my book is at least partly instructive.

The All-American Lieutenant is a story describing the noteworthy accomplishments made on battlefields and naval venues to fend off the Axis enemies determined to defeat and enslave America. The book is a fictionalized love story with events of World War II intertwined creating a literary blend sure to interest readers. The text highlights one man's patriotic quest doing all he can to help win the war, and his soldiering, courage, and sacrifice represent the best of all who served. Acknowledging and celebrating the exploits of many through the life and times of this military hero was both an honor and privilege.

Honoring the fallen, over 400,000 in number, and the thousands injured, is at the core of the book and their service cannot be overstated. Accordingly, this book is dedicated to those who gave their lives that we, as a nation, might live and relish the freedoms their efforts made possible. *God bless them*.

FOREWORD

A work of prose, a novel —usually of some length, contains a myriad of literary possibilities and normally conforms to a specific genre: mystery, romance, science fiction, fantasy, historical fiction. Author Rich Grimes chose the latter. A former history teacher, an aficionado of world wars, and a published author and researcher, he skillfully juxtaposes a love story with the military events of World War II. In the process, he pens a very compelling story in the *All-American Lieutenant*.

Eschewing length for brevity, the read is fast —an electric, page-turner laced with unease, personal tragedy, and descriptions of battlefield, air, and sea engagements. The protagonists enlist in the United States Army, threatening the existence of their seemingly irrevocable bond. The maniacal nature of the war impacts militarists and civilians alike in all parts of the globe including a small town in Minnesota, the venue where the story originates.

The author examines America's neutrality and its transformation to patriotic fervor as a result of the Japanese attack on Pearl Harbor. Thereafter, the reader will be privy to the angst confronting two families regarding the fate of their loved ones serving overseas. A chronological summary of events in both European and Pacific theatres are infused into the text to provide a parallel continuity to the plight of Lieutenant Richard James and Private Phyllis Verducci. Their very survival is problematic.

An epilogue, a unique feature at the conclusion of the book, offers a peek into the future and reveals the fate of the protagonists post-war. Grimes strikes a chord of heartache, sorrow, and death, assessing the changing complexity of relationships and how they are altered or destroyed by events over which there is no control. America and its allies win the war, but human and material costs are staggering. Readers will experience the vicissitudes of raw emotions exhibited by the characters as the story offers few happy moments. Ultimately, we learn, contrary to the popular saying, that all is NOT fair in *love* and *war*.

- W.R. Cantrell

PREFACE

Everyone, - teachers, friends, classmates and their parents, believed Richard James and Phyllis Verducci were a match made in heaven. Although this assessment might have been premature, early on the two acted like a wedding was in their future. Born to working, middle-class parents, they attended the same schools, had similar interests, and were both very athletic. They even completed each other's sentences.

Growing up in a quiet neighborhood in a small town called Elbow Lake, Minnesota, located 150 miles south of the Canadian border, they snow skied and ice skated in the winter, and swam in the many nearby lakes during the summer. With many friends in their company, the city was their playground. They did everything together. To no one's surprise, Richard starred as a three-sport athlete in high school and Phyllis captained the cheer squad. Due to their friendly, humble personalities and their athletic and academic prowess, their popularity was unmatched. The icing on the cake occurred when they were voted king and queen of their senior prom.

Richard and Phyllis graduated with honors from Elbow Lake High School in 1939. Talented in many ways, they seemed destined for success in whatever endeavors they chose. They indeed had all the "right stuff." But attending college was their first priority and they matriculated to different locations, thinking that was the best and most logical way to go. However, they remained committed to each other and often spoke of marriage. Phyllis believed waiting for their betrothal until after college was best. Richard reluctantly agreed and prior to going their separate ways, he presented his best girl a promise ring. She cried when he slipped it on her finger and said how much she loved him. They promised to write and phone and off they went. Their future was bright, or so they thought. However, a world at war would change all that.

For the better part of a decade, the United States government and the public were united in opposition to American participation in European hostilities. Neutrality was a consistent mantra, a foreign policy of isolationism spurred on by overwhelming public support. In 1936, a survey by George Gallup revealed 95% of those polled believed America should stay out of any European war. Some Americans believed Germany was merely seeking compensation to which it felt entitled as a result of its humiliating defeat in World War I and a subsequent, suffocating peace treaty. However, through 1939-40, Adolf Hitler's Wehrmacht was virtually invincible and European nations continually acquiesced to the Fuhrer, hoping somehow he would just go away. Fooled by false promises, some countries signed non-aggression pacts. But the more he acquired, the more he wanted. Intimidating nations at will, Hitler crushed all opponents and indiscriminately targeted innocent civilians, including women and children. Thousands died. His goal would soon become apparent: the domination and enslavement of Europe and eventually the rest of the world.

Despite Hitler's successes, America still balked. The general public and politicians alike anticipated England would prove to be a buffer and restore order in Europe. That was a pipe dream. Despite providing our important ally and friend with munitions, ships, and food, in 1940 England was holding on for dear life. That summer the German Luftwaffe bombed London incessantly, resulting in the deaths of hundreds of civilians. In response, the RAF retaliated, bombing Berlin. Hitler was incensed and mistakenly thought England would surrender following more frequent bombing raids of London.

But Prime Minister Winston Churchill inspired resistance and resolve, pledging to never give up. Of
tough, resilient stock, the English people endured
the bombing as courageous RAF fighter pilots and
skilled ground personnel thwarted a German air assault over England in the Battle of Britain. Under-
dogs, their efforts kept Germany at bay for the time
being.

Now Hitler had to rethink his plans. Despite
the advice of his top generals to maintain a military
posture against England, he decided to delay a land
invasion in favor of a bigger prize — the Soviet Union. Thus, he broke the non-aggression pact with
Stalin and initiated Operation Barbarossa full force
on June 22, 1941. In the beginning stages it appeared Germany would overwhelm the Russian
army. They came close but despite early military
victories, defeat was inevitable. Turns out, the determined Red Army, a brutal Russian winter, Hitler's
misguided strategies and his obsession with taking
Stalingrad coupled with strategic decision-making
blunders, doomed Germany in the eastern front.

The Japanese surprise attack on the American
naval base at Pearl Harbor, Hawaii, six months later
on Sunday, December 7, 1941, was a calamitous
event — a portend of the escalation of the war to

Asia and the South Pacific. Thousands of American seaman were killed in the surprise attack and our fleet was crippled. President Franklin D. Roosevelt addressed a joint session of Congress the next day, stating that due to the "dastardly" attack by the Japanese Imperial nation, a state of war existed between the United States and Imperial Japan. Like it or not, we were all in.

No longer a bystander, a fight of the first magnitude lie ahead. FDR's declaration of war resulted in Congress reauthorizing the draft, lowering the age of conscription to 18. Although woefully under-equipped, outmanned, and ill-prepared for combat, unanimity of purpose suddenly pervaded America. An army didn't exist. But Americans had suffered their own kind of humiliation and a wave of revenge swept the homeland. A burgeoning wave of intense nationalism inspired thousands of young men to enlist. Families, especially mothers, wives, and girlfriends, were worried sick about the fate of their loved ones. Understandably so.

Leaving their families behind, soldiers, many just teenagers, were killed in many overseas venues. However, those fortunate enough to survive returned home at war's end. Some discovered their wives or girlfriends had abandoned them. Thinking that their man was missing in action or dead, some women remarried or entered into a romantic liaison with another only to hear their husband or boyfriend knock on the door. Legal entanglements ensued.

World War II served as the flash point of this book and as background connecting the characters to a very personal, compelling story with alternating venues and some unexpected surprises. Protagonists Richard and Phyllis rode the wave of patriotism and both enlisted in the United States Army. Overseas and for the foreseeable future, their love would be put to the test.

INTRODUCTION

On a rainy Monday morning, September 30, 1945, Judge Raymond Strasser officiated the civil hearing in his private chambers at the county courthouse, the purpose of which was to examine and discuss Phyllis' petition to dissolve her marriage to Richard. Both parties were represented by counsel, Phyllis by Patrick Dowd, and Richard by Margaret Levine. Their parents waited nervously in the lobby area near the front entrance. Phyllis' sole contention was that Richard's brain impairment was impeding their ability to relate as a couple, let alone a married one. All attempts on her part to reconnect and regrow their relationship were futile. After nearly a year living apart, Richard showed no interest in her.

CHAPTER 1

On September 15, 1935, Richard woke up late, dressed, brushed his teeth, grabbed a piece of toast on his way out the door, and then turned around to give his mom, Janet, a good-bye kiss on the cheek. She smiled and told him to be careful. That is what mothers always say. His blue denim overalls were askew in the back and his shoe laces were untied, but he didn't notice, or if he did, he didn't care. Every morning on school days, Richard walked a few blocks to Michael and Cheryl Verducci's house to pick up Phyllis. They would then walk a short distance to Abraham Lincoln Junior High School.

Richard knocked on the door and Mrs. Verducci opened it and offered a warm greeting. "Come in, Richard. What's new?" Not knowing what to say, he mentioned the weather was getting cooler by the day. Cheryl agreed and stated that cold weather and snow were coming soon. Richard nodded.

Wearing a long white apron over a printed house dress, Cheryl motioned for Richard to take his usual seat at the dining room table. She normally didn't cook a big breakfast but today was Friday and she wanted to — just because. She had prepared sausage, bacon, and fresh fruit with white bread ready to toast. Phyllis entered the room looking as cute as a bug and said good morning. His manners always impeccable, Richard waited for his girlfriend to sit down. He was quite the gentleman. Cheryl smiled and took her seat. Phyllis wore a pink skirt coordinated with a freshly-pressed white blouse and white flats. Her long blonde hair was fixed in a ponytail tied by a pink ribbon, and the light make up she had applied made her face glow. Richard found it difficult not to stare. Tall with a slim physique, striking green eyes, and a dimple in her cheek, Phyllis was the picture of beauty. Richard didn't know she thought him to be the most handsome boy in town. They glanced at each other but so as not to be embarrassed, they avoided eye contact.

There was little doubt - Richard was imposing for his age. Fifteen years old, six feet tall, muscular, short brown hair in a crew cut, and large hazel eyes, his appearance was manlike. When walking the halls at school, students passing by gave him room and gawked. He exuded a presence in physical education classes, the school cafeteria, and around campus. Unknowingly charismatic, his intellect, physical size, athletic talent, and popularity endeared him to classmates, teachers, and the school administration. Everyone on campus knew he and Phyllis were a couple but females swooned over him. Although most didn't interfere with their relationship, a few tried with no success.

"Phyllis, did you do your homework last night?" Richard asked.

Smirking slightly, she helped herself to several pieces of bacon set out on the table and replied, "What do you think?"

Richard grimaced, turned to her mother, and said, "She always answers a question with a question. Does she do that to you and Mr. Verducci?"

"Richard, please call us Cheryl and Michael. But yes, that is one of her favorite conversation techniques. She tries to deflect questions to throw us off, but it doesn't work. We know her too well." Phyllis smiled.

Richard persisted, "Well, what about your homework?"

"I did it, thank you very much and I suppose you did your homework, too?"

"What do you think," he replied.

Everyone laughed and then Phyllis said, "You got me on that one."

Richard thanked Cheryl for breakfast and accompanied Phyllis to the door after gathering their belongings. School started in about half an hour so the two ninth graders got on their way. Bounding off the porch onto the front lawn, Richard extended his hands for Phyllis to embrace him, but she scampered to the sidewalk, chuckling. Richard frowned.

On many occasions on their walks to school, a delicate black and yellow hummingbird positioned himself slightly in front of the couple at eye level, wings flapping a mile a minute as if to say hello before flying away. Looking out the living room window, Cheryl often witnessed this unusual event. No wonder she referred to Richard and her daughter as "love birds." When they arrived at school, they blew each other kisses and went their separate ways.

On Sunday, Richard and Phyllis' parents attended a social at the Christian church in town.
These events comprised of an opening prayer, a
summary of community activities, a discussion —
led by a guest speaker familiar with national and
world affairs, followed by a light supper in the rec-
reation room.

The Verducci's and the James' liked these
gatherings. They were always informative and
thought-provoking. The evening's presenter, a professor and expert in American foreign policy, offered an ominous view of European politics and
predicted America would try to avoid involvement
in any foreign entanglements. But in the end, an
unforeseeable event would change that perception.
He added that Americans were still coping with the
depression, surviving day to day to support their
families. This assertion was validated by the continued high unemployment in Elbow Lake. The professor took his seat and the audience in the church
annex, around 30 in number, buzzed. Those in
agreement with his views applauded. But a few in
the audience were visibly skeptical, shaking their
heads.

An elderly woman raised her hand. Acknowledged by the moderator, she rose slowly. Most

likely in her 80's and frail, her words were clearly articulated. She said evil forces were at work in Europe and read recently in the local paper that Germany, Italy, and Japan had signed an alliance. These countries were the Axis powers. Stating emphatically, "They are undoubtedly up to no good and America will eventually be forced into a terrible world war. Sooner or later we will have to move ourselves off the sidelines and into the fray. The world is watching, hoping America will be the bulwark."

A young woman seated near her stood and said emphatically, "No!"

The elderly woman, undeterred, then stated, "Please hear me out." Continuing, she said that it was both dangerous and foolhardy that many are in denial of what is ahead. Hoping the forces of which she spoke would merely disappear of their own volition was a falsehood. "Believe you me," she said, "America is on a collision course with powerful and determined enemies. That's all I have to say."

An eerie silence fell over the room. Now dismissed to supper, the audience exited the room quietly. Janet's heart sunk, and she sensed Richard would eventually participate in a terrible conflict far from home. She kept this thought to herself and prayed silently her foreboding wouldn't come to pass.

CHAPTER 2

Fast forward. Elbow Lake experienced a mild summer in 1936 but enough hot days to lure the town's youth into Lake Millerton. Most swam and cavorted about and a few fished at the north end. They enjoyed the warm water, barbecues, and nightly fireworks. On weekends, water skiing and boating were permitted in designated areas under the supervision of lifeguards. Many incoming high school tenth graders, including Richard and Phyllis, however, spent time at school each morning during summer vacation participating in activities. Richard practiced on the Varsity football team and Phyllis the cheer squad. They would both become leaders of their respective pursuits once school opened and to no one's surprise, they excelled.

Elbow Lake High School provided a plethora of both academic and athletic activities, and most students found something they liked. Extracurricular events were well organized and school spirit was sky high. Rallies, bonfires, and spirit assemblies ignited the fall semester. A town with one high school, the community supported it in a big way and although the economy was still in recovery mode, the fundraisers conducted on behalf of the various groups netted monies enabled students to compete in scholastic competitions at neighboring schools and help pay for bus transportation. The school's budget paid for transporting athletes and coaches to away contests.

High school years flew by. Their junior year, Richard and Phyllis participated in so many school activities they could barely keep them straight. Although Phyllis' chief interest was leading the cheer squad, she branched off into another endeavor that came about by chance. In her civics class, as a result of talking with a female classmate seated next to her, Phyllis learned the girl was homeless. Consequently, Phyllis made an appointment with the school principal to discuss how she and the school could help fellow homeless students.

A committee was formed, and a plan was established to support Elbow Lake High School students unfortunate enough to be living without the basic necessities of life and in many cases in a car or public park. Of greatest concern was the brutal winter weather where temperatures often dipped below freezing, prompting health concerns for young and old. Due to confidentiality and respect for personal privacy, identifying those needing assistance was difficult. But Phyllis and a number of class-mates under the able leadership of a faculty adviser and with the involvement of local service clubs in town persisted. A community outreach program was launched. Phyllis' parents did their part and made an extremely compassionate offer, welcoming the homeless female student Phyllis befriended into their home for a few months until she was placed in foster care.

Homeless students, as well as many of the town's adult transient population, were provided food, blankets, clothing, toiletries, and private counseling. The district's junior high school and three elementary schools pitched in. Richard and his Varsity football teammates served as "runners," helping with the pickup and delivery of all the do-nated items. The last day of school, Phyllis was pre-sented a special award at an all-school assembly ac-knowledging her caring, humanitarian pursuit to help the homeless. She ushered in rays of positive energy and awareness to the school and the Elbow Lake community advocating on behalf of those in-dividuals who struggled to just survive day to day. Her efforts also earned special recognition by the city mayor at a city council meeting. Truly, Phyllis was a benevolent angel.

CHAPTER 3

Ben James was the best auto mechanic in town. Truth be told, he was the only auto mechanic. By virtue of the depressed economy other mechanics had to pull out and pursue employment elsewhere. But most locals owned a vehicle and, of course, maintenance and repairs were necessary. However, they seldom had the money to pay. In order to accommodate them and keep his business above ground, Ben offered payment plans or facilitated a barter arrangement. Bartering, a practice often successfully used in 19th century America, particularly in farming communities, was an economic system that seemed to work well, although sometimes determining the value of the exchanged goods or services was difficult. But Ben made it work and his customers were grateful. He was always seeking ways to support his family but as hard as he worked, it seemed there was always more money owed than the funds to make the payments. Neighbors and community members found themselves in the same boat.

One cold December day, Ben realized he didn't have the money to make his mortgage payment.

As a result of a previous barter agreement with a farmer, he had accepted a black and white dairy cow in exchange for repairs on his tractor. This cow, black and white with a huge head, produced goodly amounts of milk, and roamed Ben and Janet's backyard and was housed in a small barn. Possessing a quirky personality, she didn't like Janet and only allowed Ben to milk her. Thinking he could initiate another barter agreement himself, Ben walked to the bank with the cow in tow and politely inquired with a banker friend if he could barter the cow for a house payment. People in town looked on in disbelief and bank employees peered out the window to witness this most unusual transaction. One woman inside the bank said this was something you didn't see every day. It didn't take long for the banker to agree to Ben's proposal and gave him a 3- month credit on his house payment. This was a generous offer and, as was the custom in those days, they sealed the deal with a handshake. When Ben informed his wife about the arrangement, Janet, always the frugal, conscientious penny pincher, laughed out loud, hugged her husband and forced a smile.

Later, after his work day and while Janet was shopping, Ben relaxed with a cold drink on the couch. He got up and walked down the hall, stopped at a closed bedroom door, and stared at it. This was his son David's room, still intact with the bed made and all his belongings arranged neatly on shelves and in his closet. The poster of King Kong was still taped to the wall above the window. When his wife wasn't home, Ben went into the room and sat down on the bed, remembering the wonderful times they had fishing in the summer. He had a very tough time accepting his son's tragic death who succumbed to Leukemia when he was nine years old. His death devastated the family and punctured Janet's heart, thrusting her into a debilitating depression. She lost weight after David's funeral, seldom conversed, and often secluded herself in the bedroom. Grief consumed her. Ben, and to some degree, Richard, gave her their support and the family talked infrequently about his passing. Janet's behavior lightened over time while at the same time she became increasingly protective of Richard.

Ben was a hard worker, devoted to his family and business - a good man. He and Richard spent quality time together. They went fishing, made overnight trips to the mountains, and attended as many school athletic contests together as possible —high school, college, and professional. Since Janet disliked crowds, she normally stayed home. Ben supported Richard's athletic endeavors including football, basketball, and baseball and was visible in the stands at Richard's games, home and away, as his work schedule permitted. Richard revered his father and thought him very wise. Ben exhibited a high level of intelligence and emotional acumen. He seldom made judgments and posed questions when he and Richard had serious conversations, making his son put on his thinking cap. Father and son bonded in a most propitious way. Considering Ben had no formal education, he possessed qualities to which his more educated peers could only aspire — common sense and good judgment.

CHAPTER 4

Labor Day weekend 1938 signaled the end of summer and the beginning of another school year. Richard and Phyllis were now bona fide seniors. This holiday, however, had special significance. It was Ben's 50th birthday. Accordingly, Janet hosted a party in his honor. Mike and Cheryl Verducci attended, and the couples enjoyed a delicious dinner, feasting on meat loaf, Ben's favorite dish. After dinner, the celebration moved from the dining room to the parlor for coffee and cake. Richard and Phyllis showed up for the dessert and joined the adults singing Happy Birthday. Ben blew out the candles and made a wish he prayed fervently would come true.

Settled in and comfortable, the adults made small talk until to everyone's surprise, Janet posed an interesting question. "Do you guys remember the elderly woman at the church social who spoke so forcefully about America's involvement in a war?"

Stunned and initially silent, Ben, Cheryl, and Michael looked at each other. Ben broke through, stating that the church social his wife referenced had taken place a long time ago — over two years.

Janet's face turned red and suddenly became animated, a behavior defying her normally demure disposition. "Well,"? she probed, seeking an answer. Silence.

Taking Janet's hand in his, Ben spoke up. "Yes, sweetheart, I remember, and I believe the Verducci's do, too. Let's accept the reality that war is coming. It's just a matter of time." Again, silence. Cheryl then suggested that the women refresh the coffee. Now calm, Janet said, "Good."

The subject of war was not broached the rest of the evening. While in the kitchen, Cheryl ruminated about the conversation at dinner and understood Janet's fear that somehow Richard would have to fight in a war far from home. Moreover, the thought of the James' family losing another child was unthinkable.

CHAPTER 5

Senior year high school can be either be fun or a disaster. High expectations and the many activities, particularly spring semester, give way to the sudden realization that the "real world," awaited. Post-high school employment was problematic. If one had the financial resources and the grades, college was an option. But a degree didn't guarantee a job. The national economy was improving slightly so there was some cause for optimism. But Richard and Phyllis were both oblivious to the stark realities of conditions outside their own town. Who could blame them? They weren't the only seniors operating under the guise of naivete. With acute intellects, athletic and leadership skills, compassionate character, and thriving on one success after another, they seemed to have the world on a string. But late in 1939 all that would change.

Richard lead the Varsity football team to both league and state championships and college scouts attending games drooled. The team's starting quarterback for three years, he ran like a deer and passed with uncanny precision. As was the custom in most high school football programs, he played both offense and defense and intercepted opposing team's passes, running many back for touchdowns. He was heavily recruited by a number of colleges for both football and baseball and received countless letters from coaches and college admission officials in mid-western states, promising him the moon if he would only enroll. He was the first Elbow Lake High School athlete in decades to be awarded All-American status in football, an impressive honor bestowed by the Minnesota High School Athletic Federation. Of course, Richard was as thrilled as his parents were proud.

Phyllis observed Richard's exploits on the field and admired his humble disposition following the many victories his teams captured. The consummate altruist, he always gave credit to his teammates for how hard they played. Not to be outdone, Phyllis coordinated a cheer squad that won several state competitions and she placed first in the county beauty pageant three years in a row.

Their successes did not come without a price. Due to their participation in athletics and clubs, a few of their academic classes suffered. Pulling "all-nighters" to stay above water and earn respectable grades was standard operating procedure, at least

until they cut back on some of their school com-
mitments. They cruised the final quarter and were
elated when learning they had been admitted to
their colleges of choice. Phyllis insisted they attend
different collegiate venues and after some debate on
the subject, Richard agreed. More confident of their
future together, Phyllis took the high road, knowing full well that someday they would marry. Richard was less confident. He believed men at her college would be enamored by her beauty and charm
and do all they could to romance her. Although he
wasn't the jealous type, he struggled with the
thought of not being with her every day. To his
credit, he treasured their love, knowing it was not
just for here and now, but forever.

The Elbow Lake High School graduation
went off like clockwork. The class of 1939, 300
strong, marched onto the football field with Pomp
and Circumstance playing loudly on a phonograph
connected to a large speaker adjacent to their starting point as they walked up. Many of the graduates
were band members so live music was not used. Students faced the stage with parents and friends seated
behind them in the bleachers. The sun darted in
and out of menacing, dark clouds which raised and
lowered the temperature. But the graduates didn't
seem to care.

The ceremony was relatively short and as one might expect, the students paid little attention to the speakers — with one exception. Class Valedictorian Johnny Nimitz' words were inspirational. In less than 10 minutes, he spoke about the possibility of a great future for all moving forward but, like the day's weather, what lie ahead was at best unpredictable. Come what might, he stated that facing the coming days, months, and years was a serious responsibility. "Play time is behind us now," he joked. His classmates laughed. "It is time to grow up, put up, or shut up!" he shouted. "Now get out there and prove to the teachers, administration, parents, friends, community, and, importantly, yourselves, that the world is in good hands," he concluded. Richard and Phyllis, seated in the front row, stood up and initiated a cadenced handclap synchronized with shouts of "Johnny, Johnny, Johnny," which reverberated on the field, in the stands, and on stage. It was a feel-good moment.

One by one, the names of the graduates were called to the podium where they received their diplomas from the school principal, Dr. Rodney Jacobs. After the last name was called and with the new graduates back to the seats and now standing, he said, "Congratulations to all. I am proud of you and wish you well." With that final send off, the students threw their caps in the air and frenzied hugs abounded. The people in the bleachers erupted in sustained applause. Noisemakers, confetti, and balloons fueled the celebration. The graduates were now poised to take on the challenges of life after high school. Little did they know that in less than three months Europe would be at war and that their lives would be turned upside down.

CHAPTER 6

As agreed, Richard and Phyllis attended college in different states — at his mother's insistence, Richard in eastern Minnesota while Phyllis went to North Dakota. They were understandably excited, and each awarded full scholarships: Richard athletic, and Phyllis, academic. This eased the financial worries of their parents with college costs.

The two lovebirds were inseparable the summer before matriculating and spent most days at the lake. Although they looked for summer employment, none materialized and several days a week each helped their parents with household chores, errands, and yardwork. On one particularly hot and steamy day, Richard told Phyllis he would be glad when they left because the sweaty work was wearing him out. Phyllis laughed.

They said their good-byes at summer's end following a special candlelight supper at the Verducci's. Cheryl cooked a pot roast, vegetables, and baked a lemon meringue pie, Phyllis' favorite dessert. She set the dining table with her best dishes, silverware, and cloth linens. Two red candles were

placed on top of a green holiday tablecloth. In order to give the young adults alone time, Cheryl and
Michael went to the movies. On their way out the
door after Richard arrived, Michael surveyed the or-
nate table decorations, smiled, and said, "You never
do that for us?"

His wife replied quickly with friendly sar-
casm, "The next time you go away to college, I'll
make it happen."

Over dinner, Richard and Phyllis reminisced
about their high school days and discussed where
the future might take them. Neither knew what major they would choose, let alone professional ambi-
tions after graduation. But they suspected everything would fall into place. It always had.

After they devoured several pieces of Cheryl's
pie, they started to clear the table and do the dishes.
When Phyllis went into the kitchen, she saw a sign
taped across the sink which read: Don't you dare!
Enjoy each other and don't clean up. Your father
and I will do it. Hearing her chuckle, with a few
dirty dishes in hand, Richard entered the kitchen,
read the sign, and shook his head. "You have great
parents," he said.

Phyllis replied, "Indeed I do." They followed Cheryl's instructions but cleared the table, the least they could do.

Now seated on the porch holding hands, Phyllis turned to Richard and said, "I will miss you my sweet boy and think of you every minute." She touched her promise ring and began to tear up.

Richard then stated, "You are a darling girl, beautiful inside and out, and I love you very much. How did I get so lucky?"

Phyllis kissed him on the cheek and said she was the lucky one. After an extended silence, Phyllis commented that they had been together almost every day since kindergarten. But now she was already experiencing a void — a kind of sick feeling. "I will write often and call when I can," she said. Richard said he would do the same. Phyllis cried as she rested her head on Richard's shoulder. He stroked her face.

Knowing they were leaving the next day and had to pack, they kissed good night. Richard headed for the sidewalk and Phyllis gazed at him, holding her hands over her face. Suddenly, she ran after him and jumped on his back. Once untangled, they embraced again. It was now Richard's turn to cry and Phyllis wiped away his tears. They decided to turn around, count to three slowly, and walk away. The next day their parents drove them to their respective colleges. It was September 1, 1939, the day Germany invaded Poland to begin World War II. Europe was now at war and the United States' stance of neutrality was in jeopardy. Consequently, thousands of American young men and women would be pressed into service.

CHAPTER 7

The dorm room was smallish as was Richard's roommate, Henry. Standing side by side, they resembled David and Goliath. Richard was a kind soul and over time developed great respect for Henry's intellect and easygoing personality. The young men were a compatible pair.

Henry was born and raised in Palm Desert, California, and chose a collegiate venue purposely to extricate himself from the hot desert and to get away from his overbearing mother. However, the extreme winter weather caught him off guard. When classes started in September, the conditions were mild, but Richard warned Henry it wouldn't last long. Sure enough, late October brought cold temperatures and even a few snow flurries. The temperature dipped from the 60's down to near freezing. Henry heeded Richard's prognostication and stocked up on winter clothing and stayed indoors as much as possible. Venturing out for afternoon classes sporting a wool cap, earmuffs and mittens, his breath exhaled a cold vapor. Once in the dorm, he adjusted the wall heater to high and went to bed nightly sleeping under layers of covers wearing a sweat top and bottom with two pairs of socks. Over time, he adapted to the weather. While unpacking a suitcase one day, he pulled out a pair of summer shorts and a bathing suit his mother had packed. He laughed out loud and showed his wears to Richard who echoed the guffaw. Richard, on the other hand, had adapted over the years to the cold weather and most days, even in the notoriously cold months of December and January, wore jeans, a T-shirt, and a light jacket.

Six hundred miles away, Phyllis joined a campus tour of her college with fellow freshmen, familiarizing the participants with its geography which included classroom locations, dormitories, library, cafeteria, gymnasium, and administrative offices. Phyllis had recently settled in to her dormitory room but, unlike the other females on the floor, no roommate was present. Gregarious by nature, beautiful, and intelligent, Phyllis introduced herself at a co-ed dormitory mixer the day after she moved in and was immediately recognized as a terrific young woman. A male student was smitten by her charm and asked her out on a date, but she respectfully declined. Several peers volunteered to become her roommate. Of course, Phyllis was flattered but the Resident Director shared with her dormmates that her roommate, Maya, was in transit and would arrive in a few days. An international student from South Africa, she was temporarily detained by customs officials at the Pretoria airport. In the meantime, Phyllis acclimated herself to new surroundings and concluded this is where she should be. Missing Richard was a constant, but she knew their college choices and temporary separation were for the best.

For Richard and Phyllis, fall semester at their respective schools was diametrically different from their high school experience. Both studied hard but struggled to earn B grades. Academically, college was a different animal. The demands of each class were compounded by stiff competition from fellow students. It didn't matter much where you attended high school or what you did there. It was all about here and now. Lecture halls were governed by erudite, strict, and in some cases, uncompromising professors. They talked throughout class time and elicited little in the way of questions or comments from the students. This method, unlike the Socratic system of give and take emphasizing discussion and self-discovery employed by many of Richard and Phyllis' high school teachers, was the standard modus operandi. Blue book exams often contained complex questions requiring depth and clarity of written expression, challenging to say the least.

Phyllis was ill on and off most of the first term, adversely affecting her energy, attendance, and grades. Richard didn't fare much better. His grades halfway through the semester averaged a C+ and he had to work at it to achieve these marks. In high school, he earned mostly A's and with few exceptions breezed through his classes without much effort. Studying was hit and miss. But those days were over. To make matters worse, he suffered a season-ending injury quarterbacking in the first football game — a separation in his left shoulder that required wearing a sling. Fortunately, the injury was in his non-throwing shoulder, so rest and proper rehabilitation would enable him to return to play football the next season. Richard took this setback in stride and roamed the sidelines in the subsequent games — clipboard in hand, chiefly to record yards gained by his team's offense. His coaches and teammates were impressed with his work ethic and loyalty. Thankfully, he retained his athletic scholarship.

True to her word, Phyllis wrote Richard often and kept a handkerchief close by to contain a dripping nose, cough, and sneezing. Her health was not good, but she managed to convey a positive outlook. She counted the days until the holidays when she and Richard could spend time together at home. Richard called Phyllis every Friday from a pay phone located in the lobby of his dormitory. He had to phone early in the morning since many of his dorm mates queued up behind him, change in hand. During their conversations, the couple commiserated regarding their struggles and set-backs. They encouraged each other and believed things would eventually improve.

School newspapers at both campuses covered college events and much of the copy addressed the war in Europe with news features and editorials. The editors at both schools supported America's neutrality and believed England could defeat Hitler without American help. That was unlikely.

Richard's World Civilization professor, Dr. William Clark, an accomplished lecturer, researcher, and author, taught about the notable people, places, and events occurring from the 16th century on. However, doing so with any degree of thoroughness was impossible. He knew it and so did the students. When lecturing about the European turmoil lead-ing up to and including the mayhem and madness of World War I, he stated that following the war unemployment in Germany created political instability and widespread anger over the terms of the peace treaty ending the conflict, punishing the Fatherland. The seeds of yet another world calamity were sown. All this gave rise to one Adolph Hitler.

Despite all the historical doom and gloom of wars, famine, religious infighting, political corruption, and rise and fall of monarchies, the students - especially Richard, enjoyed Dr. Clark's upbeat instructional style. They admired and respected his wit, wisdom, and outgoing personality. His descriptions of Germany ravaging Europe in real time created a tension adding to the unrest and anxiety already present on campus. Many students at the college (although few expressed it openly) believed history would repeat itself and America would once again, as in the intervention in World War I, be forced to save the day. The war in Europe was spreading.

Richard paid Dr. Clark a visit in his office the day following the final World Civilization exam. The holiday break was approaching, and Richard wanted to ask the professor a question or two. Once inside the small office, he nearly choked. Dr. Clark smoked cigars, one after another, and the haze and pungent smell permeated the breathable air. Richard's face was turning green, so the good professor opened the window and waved his hands wildly about to clear the smoke in the air. The two sat and before Richard spoke, Dr. Clark said, "I think I know why you are here and it's not to discuss your grade on the final."

Richard replied, "Well, now that you mention it, did you grade my blue book?"

The professor nodded, worked his way through a stack of blue books, and handed Richard his test. On the inside cover, a grade of B+ was written.

Smiling, Richard said, "Gee, this is the highest grade I have received this term in any class. Thank you." His teacher smiled and said he had earned it. Richard explained he was worried about the war in Europe and feared he and many of his friends would be drafted. He wanted to know if he thought America would enter the conflict.

Dr. Clark, not one to offer biased views or unsubstantiated assumptions, queried, "What do you think?"

Richard smiled and meaning no disrespect, stated that answering a question with a question was a technique his girlfriend often used.

Silent momentarily, Dr. Clark gave the question thought and offered a definitive response. He surmised President Roosevelt would likely provide munitions, even ships, to help alleviate England's burden but not resort to committing troops. However, he said that events could change, resulting in alteration of military policy. "Does this help, Richard?" His protege said yes.

The meeting ended with the two men discussing holiday plans. The professor planned to remain in town with his wife and his children and grandchildren would spend Christmas with them. Richard said he looked forward to going home to Elbow Lake where he could rest, relax, and socialize with family and girlfriend. Coughing and now experiencing a headache, Richard stood and said he appreciated his professor's time but had to leave —before the cigar smoke killed him. They laughed, shook hands, and said good-bye.

CHAPTER 8

The holidays provided a much welcome respite for Richard and Phyllis. Spending virtually every waking moment together - in addition to Christmas shopping, ice skating, and attending parties with high school friends they continued a tradition cutting down trees for their respective homes. Decorating them was a festive activity reminiscent of Christmases past, with family members pitching in. Positive feelings about Richard and Phyllis being home added to the good cheer. Outside, the weather was freezing, and traces of snow dotted the neighborhood, but each home warmed things up with fireplaces blazing. This holiday, however, was clouded by daily reports in local newspapers, mostly bad, about the war in Europe. No one wanted to discuss it, hoping that somehow Germany would be neutralized and make peace. But Hitler was seizing territories at will and for the most part with little resistance.

The day before Richard and Phyllis traveled back to school, they decided to have alone time and walked to a local cafe for lunch where they had a serious conversation. First on their minds was the hardship they were experiencing being apart for months at a time and what, if anything, to do about it. Withdrawing from school, for either of them, was not an option. Their parents would be crushed and considering future professional endeavors, made no sense. Writing and calling more often was a good idea, albeit a band aid. Richard said he wanted to play baseball in the spring but knew the time involved was an important commitment. Weekend games would preclude visiting Phyllis.

Once the subject was brought up, Phyllis asked, "Why wouldn't you play baseball? Next to football, that is your best sport."

Richard replied, "To be with you, silly."

Phyllis said that being with her, except during holidays or spring breaks, was not practical due to her busy school schedule. The distance between them would require Richard take a bus since he didn't have a car. The cost in time and travel was prohibitive. Richard shrugged his shoulders and put his head down.

He then offered an irrational, pie-in-the-sky possibility. "I will enroll at your school and play football. We could study and be together."

Phyllis smiled, put both her hands in his and said that wouldn't work, at least for her. "Besides, we don't have a football team." Richard forced a laugh. At this moment, it was all he could do NOT to propose marriage. Phyllis then looked directly into his eyes and asked, "What?" Richard shook his head.

They ate lunch in total silence, but their minds were in spin mode. Their good-bye the next day was not as dramatic or humorous as the one they had when they initially left for college; it was downright somber. But their moods lightened slightly when they arrived home and accessed their mail containing fall semester grades. Phyllis was very surprised but happy she earned an A, three B's and a C+. Richard pulled a B+ in World Civilization, three B's and a C. He wasn't thrilled, but his marks were higher than he expected.

Spring semester went very well for Richard and Phyllis, especially their academics. Trying to learn the ins and outs of studying and succeeding in college by themselves was not proving to be fruitful. Accordingly, they joined study groups. Richard was invited to participate in a so-called elite organization comprised of campus nerds who relished out-smarting the professors. At first, Richard thought these fellows a bit sleazy and was disgusted with their foul body odor. Apparently, they kept themselves busy studying rather than bathing. But these oddballs were very intelligent and results-oriented. Richard went along for the ride and couldn't resist poking fun at them. For the second session, Richard showed up to one of their "secret" study venues wearing a mask. He made his point and they snickered. One of the nerds interrupted a sip on a soft drink and belched loudly. At the mid-term grading period, Richard earned his best grades to date and was very happy. If he received equally high marks by the end of the semester, he would make the honor roll.

Phyllis pledged for one of the many college sororities spring semester and endured the obligatory hazing to gain full membership. A sorority tradition was to provide support, mentoring, and academic tutoring to any member wishing to participate. Phyllis gladly signed on and found the study groups to be both serious and helpful. The sorority sisters in her group - mostly upper-class women, knew the ropes, especially the idiosyncratic tendencies of most of the professors, the types of tests they gave, and their methods of grading. Now with an appreciation of what to study, Phyllis learned rapidly how to study. Like Richard, her grades at the mid-term were excellent and she too seemed destined for academic honors.

Knowing how to budget their time for academic study, Richard and Phyllis now could devote themselves to a few social activities. Richard's study group, as one might expect, eschewed socializing but his buddies on the football team showed him the way. Although at the many "underground" parties alcohol was readily available, Richard abstained. At these events he met several attractive females who couldn't keep their eyes off him. He resisted their advances as best he could save one extremely attractive freshman female, Donna Frieband, who rivaled Phyllis in beauty, intellect, and personality. Their friendship was platonic and openly shared with each other that they had a special friend attending another college. Initially, they dated casually but as time passed, they found it difficult not to take things further. Richard found himself between a rock and a hard place but remained wholeheartedly devoted to Phyllis.

The balance of the school year was largely uneventful. Due to a genuine commitment to academics, they worked their way to a consistent and rewarding level of achievement and settled in to a steady routine of attending classes, utilizing the library, and participating in their respective study groups. Richard excelled on the baseball team after a successful rehabilitation of his injured shoulder while Phyllis, much to the surprise of family and friends, made the woman's volleyball team. Choosing to participate in a sport rather than cheer for it was a departure for Phyllis but the newness of it suited her, and the physicality involved kept her in good shape. Richard supported, in fact, encouraged her athletic endeavor.

During the season, Phyllis worked hard to improve the various skills needed for success and, as a result, actual playing time increased during the matches. The young assistant volleyball coach, Jerome Barnhart, two years her senior, worked with Phyllis after practices, and an infatuation developed. They went out on a few dates, but Phyllis remained fiercely loyal to Richard. It was now painfully obvious that the relationship between the two lovebirds was slowly changing. But neither saw the harm spending time with other people.

CHAPTER 9

College students in the summer of 1940 sought employment and for the most part, prospects were bleak. Across the Atlantic Ocean, England valiantly defended itself to withstand German bombing. Thousands perished as the reign of aerial terror ravaged London. As history recounts, these attacks were part of an eventful time described as England's Darkest Hour, beginning with the fall of France in June 1940, and ending with the German invasion of the Soviet Union in June, 1941 — a long, excruciatingly frightful 363 days. Prime Minister Winston Churchill, ever the bulldog and inspiration for the English people, expressed a determined nation's commitment to resist in a speech on June 4, 1940.

He said, "We shall fight on the seas and the oceans. We shall fight on the beaches. We shall fight in the fields and in the streets. We shall fight in the hills....and will carry the struggle until in God's good time, the New World, will all its power and might, steps forth to the rescue and the liberation of the Old. Even though large tracts of Europe and many old and famous states have fallen or may fall into the grip of the Gestapo and all the odious apparatus of Nazi rule, we shall not flag or fail." Hailed as the chief antagonist against Hitler, his words were an anthem and harbinger of English resolve.

Despite the neutrality to which America still clung, continuing that posture would soon be a noose around its geopolitical neck. Millions of innocent civilians in Europe were suffering and countless were fleeing their Nazi tormentors when and where they could. Newspapers throughout America covered and reported on the Battle of Britain extensively thanks to cable communications from the English overseas press office in London. Many Americans remained indifferent to the plight of their sworn ally while a growing number were resigned to the inevitability of United States involvement in Europe. College students were becoming increasingly concerned. Richard was outwardly nervous. Civil dialogue morphed into heated debate in public venues, college campuses, church socials, athletic events and parlors in homes across America. Opposing views were whispered in libraries. Barber shops were a particular hotbed of conversation. The winds of fortune and war were changing and even the most recalcitrant opponents of intervention were having second thoughts.

Once Richard and Phyllis adapted to the rigors of college life, they settled in and learned to appreciate both the academic and social aspects. However, Richard became increasingly concerned about being drafted. A football teammate shared that once America entered the war, the Selective Service System would enact the draft of males 18-years of age and older. He obtained this information from his father, a captain in the United States Army, who seemed to know his stuff. Richard wanted to learn more about the draft and how it might affect him. Consequently, during Christmas break he paid a local Army recruitment center a visit near Elbow Lake. A somewhat gruff Master Sergeant laid it out and pulled no punches. He asserted that once America entered the war, and they would enter, massive manpower would be needed to defeat Germany. Although not officially announced in late 1940, President Roosevelt planned to instruct Congress to authorize the draft and did so immediately following the Japanese attack on Pearl Harbor.

Richard asked the Sergeant what he thought he should do. "Enlist as soon as possible," shouted the man loudly with a bit of a smirk on his face. He believed Richard's intellect, athletic skill, and college experience enhanced the possibility of acceptance into officer candidate school, preferably in the Army. Richard was now armed with what he considered reliable information which would help eventually in making an intelligent decision about military service. In the meantime, however, he would wait until events unfolded overseas. So as not to worry his family and Phyllis, he didn't share what he learned from the sergeant at the recruitment center. Of course, eventually Richard and Phyllis' parents, except Richard's mother, would be privy to his dilemma and supported his desire to defend America from hostile enemies.

CHAPTER 10

American military intelligence missteps at the highest levels and diplomatic bungling precipitated, and in the view of many - facilitated the successful Japanese attack on Pearl Harbor, Hawaii on December 7, 1941. An unexpected, catastrophic event, the planned and systematic Japanese assault sunk or badly damaged six of the eight battleships in the U.S. Pacific Fleet and destroyed most of the Army Air Corps planes. Over 2,400 men were killed. Ending in an instant western isolationism, the attack shocked the world. A full-blown world war had begun.

Richard and Phyllis had just completed final exams when the news of the attack spread at their respective schools. In her dorm room, Phyllis sat with her head in her hands, sobbing. Richard was speechless. Once home, their families gathered at Phyllis' house, stunned. Anxious and worried, especially for Richard's well-being, they vented one by one, and eventually sat in silence. The mood was somber, and Janet retreated to Cheryl's bedroom, crying.

As anticipated, shortly after the news of the event was public knowledge, President Roosevelt directed Congress to pass a new Selective Service Act extending the draft to men ages 18-38. Richard knew he soon had to make a decision and believed if he enlisted his chances of becoming an officer were favorable. Ready to rally against America's enemies, Richard knew he would have to summon up courage and grit and face the music. Phyllis, her parents, and Richard's parents, particularly his mother, were scared but also enraged about the deaths of Americans at Pearl Harbor. However, they knew the threat to their safety and that of millions of Americans was real. Uncertain, troubling times were ahead.

Although Richard and Phyllis had originally agreed to marry after college graduation, the outbreak of hostilities, first in Europe and then the Pacific, changed their plans. Richard enlisted in the Army a few months after the Japanese attack rather than waiting to be drafted. A colonel spoke with Richard at the recruitment center and encouraged him to apply to officer candidate school after completing basic training. He did so. Possessing the personal qualities, intellect, and athleticism needed to lead men, he was prepared for the rigors and challenges of military leadership.

CHAPTER 11

The wedding of Richard and Phyllis turned out to be a disappointing affair. Hastily organized due to Richard's imminent departure, the guests exhibited a variety of emotions, from sadness to joy to anxiety. But they put on happy faces to support the loving couple. Knowing Richard and Phyllis' parents and appreciative of the work both did on behalf of the homeless students at the high school a few years earlier, city mayor John Bloomfield and his wife, Nora, hosted the wedding at their mansion outside of town. The ceremony was conducted in the early afternoon outside adjacent to a large gazebo on a large, well-manicured lawn. Family and a few close friends were in attendance and everyone enjoyed the bright sunlight and the brevity of the proceedings. Richard and Phyllis glowed — accentuating the groom's white tuxedo and the bride's pink dress. Happy as could be, they looked like royalty. Their vows, barely audible, was a poem Phyllis wrote — a tribute to their long journey together containing words of hope, undying love, building a life, and raising a family.

The wedding reception lacked the normal celebratory tone, as those in attendance were not living in normal times with war being waged across two oceans. The festivities were abbreviated. Richard and Phyllis left for a short honeymoon not far from home. A dear couple, Mike and Jane Acosta, high school friends, drove the newlyweds to and from the hotel where the friends spent the weekend. Richard had to report to Ft. Riley, Kansas immediately after their honeymoon — a 30-hour train ride. Sad to leave his wife and family behind, he was determined to do all he could to serve and defend the country he loved.

Upon return from their honeymoon, Richard and Phyllis had to experience yet another tearful good-bye. Richard withdrew from college but encouraged his new wife to continue her studies. Extremely upset about his departure and the dangers to which he would be exposed, she wasn't ready to decide the disposition of her immediate future. Realizing that living with her parents would provide emotional support and a sense of security, she considered doing it, at least temporarily.

Phyllis drove Richard in her father's car to the train station and once there, Richard checked in. They sat in silence in the waiting area and Richard put his arm around his wife. They didn't speak for a few minutes, but Phyllis told her husband to be careful and to write as often as he could. Not knowing when they would see each other again added to the uncertainty clouding Richard's departure and dampened their farewell. But they accepted he had to leave. The future of their relationship was now up in the air and Richard wanted to focus on his commitment to defend America from all enemies. Softly, following the announcement that his train was now ready for departure, Richard said, "I will be back, sweetheart."

Phyllis, tearful, looked at him straight in his eyes saying, "I love you so much." They embraced. Richard boarded, looked out the window and waved to Phyllis. She reciprocated and as the train slowly pulled away, she sobbed. At this moment, rain began to fall.

On the long train ride, Richard ruminated about how he could help avenge the slaughter of so many unsuspecting, fellow American servicemen in Hawaii. Dying in battle in a fair fight was one thing but the premeditated Japanese attack was cowardly, he thought. Defeating imperial Japan was paramount but Richard knew German victories in Europe and their designs on extended territorial expansion had to be confronted. Richard didn't care where he was sent after the nine-week training. He just wanted to fight.

CHAPTER 12

Sleepless nights — tossing and turning, sweating, headaches - were a regular occurrence. Since Richard left, Phyllis struggled to function. Fatigued with bags under her eyes, she lost weight and her appetite. She just wasn't herself. Exhausted mentally, her general health was deteriorating. Although living with her parents was comforting and necessary, at least for the time being, she distanced herself and stayed in her bedroom. She could barely drag herself to supper and wasn't up to conversing. To make matters worse, weeks had passed, and she had yet to hear from Richard. She knew he was occupied daily with training and most likely had no time to write. Phyllis was distraught. Cheryl and Michael Verducci were beside themselves and at a loss of what to do. Their daughter was coming apart before their very eyes. It was approaching Valentine's Day, 1942.

Far away in Kansas, Richard was enduring the physical and mental challenge of his life. Master Sergeant Julius Caperton, a mean, overbearing, experienced drill instructor, coordinated the training of a contingent of twenty new U.S. Army recruits.

He was as tough as nails and seemed to enjoy tormenting the neophytes day and night. Thankfully, Richard was in excellent condition and managed to do all that was asked —coping with constant personal harassment and ridicule. He felt he had a target on his back. The sergeant recognized Richard's superior skills and intellectual aptitude and went out of his way to break him. Drill instructors do this, particularly to the strong recruits, hoping to toughen them up or wash them out.

A choreographed confrontation between the two occurred the first week. Knowing Richard was an outstanding athlete, the sergeant asked him if he was fleet of foot. He said, "Sir, yes sir." Then Caperton challenged him to a race outside the barracks. In typical Army fashion, Richard was set up to lose. The sergeant commanded Richard to pump out 100 push-ups and run the difficult obstacle course before they raced. The sergeant won but not by much. Richard's fellow soldiers cheered loudly for him and a few of the more courageous booed the sergeant for rigging the race.

Caperton just smiled. Richard's punishment for finishing second was cleaning toilets in the latrine with a toothbrush late that evening while everyone slept. But his resilience and strength were rock-hard. Half way through basic training, the sergeant completed a required progress report on his troops to the commanding officer, Lieutenant Colonel Jess Hargrove. He assessed Richard to be the best recruit of the lot who demonstrated the tenacity, aggression, skill, and leadership worthy of an Army officer.

As the training was 24-7, there was all work — lots of it, and no play. The sergeant never let up. Initially, he picked on Richard, but after the race, he focused on weak-minded recruits to humiliate. Several of these men deserted one night, were captured soon thereafter and then housed in the brig. Their ultimate fate was not known but Richard suspected each would face serious consequences and jail time.

In the minds of the recruits, time stood still and the sergeant berating them seemed endless. Fortunately, they were fed three meals a day, and during that time no one bothered them. One particularly cruel practice interrupted sleep in the middle of the night followed by maneuvers where live ammunition was employed. Consequently, Richard and his fellow soldiers learned quickly to keep their heads down.

Once the maneuvers ended and back in the barracks, it wasn't long until the men were directed to the field again. Sweating and exhausted beyond measure, they obeyed the order and managed to do what was asked. While in France two years later, Richard recalled how tired he was during these exercises but grateful the training prepared him for similar conditions in actual battle. Despite the contempt he felt for Sergeant Caperton, there was a method to his madness designed to prepare everyone in his charge to fight to withstand the rigors of battle.

Unexpectedly, one morning the sergeant allowed the men to sleep past 5 a.m. and ordered each to use an hour to write home. Richard thought this was some kind of trick, but it turned out this practice was implemented to boost morale which now was practically nonexistent. Richard quickly composed two letters, one to Phyllis and the other to his parents. At 6 a.m., everyone quick-stepped to breakfast.

The last week of basic training was purposely intense. Realizing conditions in a hostile, overseas venue would be unpredictable and life-threatening, the exercises were elevated in real-time day and night to duplicate, if at all possible, conditions they would face in battle. Richard rose to the occasion and proved to be an able, impromptu leader.

Day 63 didn't come a minute too soon for the weary recruits and a short ceremony outside the barracks honored them. Sergeant Caperton managed a smile while he shook hands with his men and pinned each with a medal. However excited, relieved if you will, Richard slept the next two days, waiting for word of his deployment. Little did he know he would be sent to Officer Candidate School at Fort Benning, Georgia on February 24, 1942. A new, different type of training awaited him.

Back in Elbow Lake, the Verducci and James families conversed often about Richard and Phyllis and shared a mutual concern about Phyllis' state of mind affecting her mental health. Just when things seemed darkest, a letter from Richard was placed in the mailbox while Phyllis was walking the family dog. When Cheryl snatched the letter out, she promptly held it up and waved it towards her daughter who was nearing the house. Cheryl handed the letter to Phyllis and then corralled the dog who was about to run free.

Phyllis read the letter in her bedroom over and over. Richard was not long on words but reassured her he was fine, although the training was more rigorous than he expected. He stated he loved her more than life itself. Phyllis used several tissues to wipe the tears running down her face. Suddenly, she was overcome with a peace and a sense of optimism she had not felt for months. His letter did much to alleviate her depressed state of mind and she thanked God to receive his welcome correspondence.

CHAPTER 13

Phyllis learned a few weeks later that Richard had been accepted to Officer Candidate School. She and her parents, not at all surprised, knew he possessed leadership qualities but were collectively concerned about his combat vulnerability. As a leader of men, he would be exposed to possible injury or death, especially in forward areas or behind enemy lines. The rank of officers in the field was identified by white squares on their helmets, making them targets of enemy snipers. As a result, countless first and second lieutenants were killed, leaving non-commissioned troops in charge, often resulting in chaos and confusion in the ranks.

Slowly, Phyllis accepted the fact her husband would be away, most likely overseas, for long periods of time. Perhaps years. In the meantime, she had to decide how she would spend her time. Her parents urged returning to college to earn a degree.

Phyllis felt safe being home and wanted to maintain contact with local high school female friends. Working part-time was her preference. Her father-in-law helped make that happen. Knowing many townspeople who frequented his repair shop, one customer made it known he was looking for someone to work weekends in his gift shop. All it took was a short interview in which Phyllis demonstrated her ebullient personality a job offer was made. Providing a mental diversion and occupying time, she performed exceedingly well in her new endeavor and in a few months was asked to work five days a week. Phyllis gladly accepted.

CHAPTER 14

At his new training venue in Georgia, Richard experienced a different kind of education. Whereas basic training was more brawn than cerebral, Officer Candidate School focused on the many aspects of leadership as well as the use of a multiplicity of armaments. Field strategies and survival skills were taught and fine-tuned. Life on the base was relatively routine and predicable on a nine to five schedule except weekends. The officers in charge, unlike Sergeant Caperton in Kansas, were polished, highly educated men — athletic, tan, intelligent and well-conditioned. They treated the officer candidates with a modicum of respect and for the most part as equals.

On Saturday and Sunday, the trainees had free time and were encouraged to participate in team sports such as volleyball, football, basketball, or baseball. Boxing was also an option. Richard stood out as one of the most highly skilled athletes and encountered a lot of competition. Turns out, however, he wasn't the only All-American soldier in camp. Organized team sports were a great diversion and a physical challenge. The supervising officers rated each man on skills, endurance, and physical agility, and made it known the best among them could exercise a most interesting service option. Those in this elite group, if selected, could play games in all parts of the globe where American soldiers were deployed. Nice work if you could get it. Simply put, these men played for pay — professional military sportsmen, if you will. Their involvement in many different locations provided a needed respite for battle-weary troops. Richard, fully qualified, was encouraged to join this noncombat sports group, but declined. His superior officers appreciated his sincere commitment fighting with the majority of fellow soldiers in actual combat.

The twelve-week officer training program flew by. All but two of the 129 candidates passed muster. Richard was one of the top candidates and was revered by his fellow soldiers for his dedication and skill performing a myriad of tasks and for supporting them when they underperformed or were saddened by an affliction to which everyone could relate. Home sickness.

The Officer Candidate Commissioning ceremony was spectacular. Conducted on a beautiful lawn at the east end of the vast training facility, the base commander pulled out all the stops: a dress parade of all the new officer recipients at the outset marching lock step to the music of a talented Army band. Speeches — most short, were inspiring. A roll call by name and presentation of their officer epaulets and medals followed by a lavish reception in the officer's mess hall were highlights. Taking place on a Saturday under bright sun light, the ceremony was well attended - mainly parents, wives, girlfriends, base Army brass, local newspaper reporters, and a few new officer candidates. Phyllis, her parents, and Richard's parents attended and they cheered loudly when Richard's name was called. Now it was official. He was a commissioned second Lieutenant in the United States Army.

Richard grinned ear to ear and saluted the presenting officer on the grandstand and the American flag. He waved to his family and stood in front of his seat near the dais. After the last honoree took his place, the base commander commended them all for a job well done and wished each success defending their country. Right on cue, hats were thrown in the air to deafening applause from the crowd. It was May 14, 1942.

This was the first time in months Richard and Phyllis had seen each other and at the reception they were inseparable. When the opportunity presented itself, they kissed and hugged like there was no tomorrow. When they had a private moment in an ante room, Phyllis was excited to learn Richard and his fellow officers were granted four days of liberty before shipping out to their assignments in the states or overseas. Staying on base, Richard, Phyllis, and their families enjoyed special time catching up and socializing, but privately Richard's parents expressed fears of the dangers he would face, wherever he was sent. Phyllis' parents were of the same opinion.

Another surprise Richard shared with everyone was that he would be deployed to Hawaii, of all places. "Why there," Phyllis asked. Apparently, Richard's outstanding work during training didn't go unnoticed. He explained that a request was made on his behalf from the senior officer at Hickam Army Air Force base, Lt. Colonel John Seacrest, who needed a top-notch assistant.

Hickam air field suffered extensive damage during the Japanese attack on Pearl Harbor. Many aircraft were destroyed including B-17 bombers. Nearly 200 men were killed on or near the air field.

Lacking knowledge of Army Air Force policies and procedures and aviation in general, Richard seemed an unlikely candidate for his new assignment. But a short interview before the commissioning ceremony with Colonel Seacrest convinced him Richard was the man for the job. Seacrest felt that Richard's intellect and leadership would enhance the rebuilding of the air base, already under construction.

Richard said, "Honey, I am a dirt dog and want to keep my feet on the ground, but this is a unique opportunity and I am all in."

Smiling, Phyllis nodded in agreement, put her head on his shoulder, rose up and whispered, "Aloha!"

CHAPTER 15

Janet James was breathing artificially from an oxygen tank and several IV's provided life-sustaining nourishment. Eyes closed, her face was as white as a sheet. She had collapsed in the kitchen while her husband was eating dinner in the dining room. Calm and collected, Ben laid her down on the sofa and called an ambulance. In less than 10 minutes, he watched the emergency crew wheel her on a gurney to the back of the ambulance. Ben jumped in and held her hand on the way to the hospital. Once there, the diagnosis was undeniable. Mrs. James had suffered a stroke.

After Janet was seen by a physician and pronounced stable, Ben phoned the Verducci's who drove immediately to the hospital. He thought it best not to contact Richard until he knew more about his mother's condition.

Two weeks prior to her son's commissioning, Janet told Ben she wasn't feeling well, complaining of headaches and fatigue. Ben told her she needed to see the family doctor but, ever stubborn, she resisted and when she said, "No means no," Ben backed off. At bedtime most nights she expressed her concerns about Richard's safety. Ben listened. Like his son, he was strong and accepted the obvious dangers inherent with his military service. On the plus side, he felt Richard's assignment in Hawaii would, at least for a time, keep him out of harm's way. After all, thousands of American soldiers would never participate in actual combat. Softly, Ben told Janet that worrying excessively about their son was not productive. But he was unable to assuage her fears.

Sitting alone in the waiting room, he surmised his wife's stroke could have been caused by the self-inflicted stress she was experiencing by fretting constantly about Richard's safety. For a few days, Janet remained in a state of semi-consciousness but was monitored continuously by a great team of nurses. Periodically, she tried to turn over and batted her eyes. Ben was forced to close his shop and spent day and night at the hospital, sleeping on an uncomfortable chair in her room surrounded by the extensive medical apparatus keeping his wife alive. On the third day, he had a long conversation with the attending physician and a consulting neurologist about Janet's condition. They explained in some detail that stroke victims are often incapacitated and fully or partially paralyzed. Their

motor, cognitive, and language functions are compromised but neither doctor knew which part of Janet's brain was impaired. Tests would be ordered in
a few days. Ben was slightly encouraged because he
learned during the conversation that some stroke
victims fully recover while others experience long-
term symptoms. Many fall somewhere in-between.
Time, rehabilitative exercises, and patient attitude
are essential components for recovery. Ben believed
his wife could recover - that is, if she wanted to.
Negative, pessimistic behaviors were obstacles to her
mental and physical health.

It didn't take long for Ben's neighbors, the
Verducci family, and churchgoers to come to his assistance. Although he was a bit overwhelmed by
their sheer numbers, he was grateful for the daily
support they offered. Captained by Michael Verducci, they organized shifts to stay with Ben at the
hospital, provide meals, and persuaded him to go
home and rest. He resisted that idea at first but after a week he was exhausted and let them help. He
knew there wasn't much he could do for his wife
and after much soul-searching, re-opened his shop
Monday through Thursday. Phyllis was a great help.
She was at the hospital early every morning, talked
to the nurses, and volunteered to do whatever
might help her mother-in-law. She stayed until

lunchtime and then worked at the gift shop in the afternoon. This was her daily routine, except weekends, for the duration of Janet's extensive stay at the hospital. It was during this period of time she met a young man, Lawrence, at a church social with whom she became infatuated. Maintaining her loyalty to Richard was foremost but Phyllis saw no harm in having male companionship. However, as one might expect, Lawrence wanted more out of the relationship than Phyllis could or was willing to give.

Meanwhile, Ben and Richard spoke almost every night and prayed together. Lt. James requested a short leave to see his mother, but his boss declined. Although Colonel Seacrest was sympathetic to Richard's plight, he simply couldn't approve leaves for soldiers under his command who had sick or dying family members. Considering the nature and urgency of war, this policy was followed by all branches of the military and made perfect sense.

CHAPTER 16

Mentored by a seasoned and knowledgeable professional officer, Richard was learning much about a variety of tasks — engineering, communication, aviation, and the coordination of Army Air Forces with ground troops. To no one's surprise, Richard was a quick study. In a short period of time, he worked independently and mastered his assigned duties. However, he felt like a fish out of water. His basic and OCS training taught him theory, elevated his physical skills, and enhanced best practices in preparation for combat on land. He preferred to lead men rather than monitor airplane schedules though. In Hawaii, he was nowhere near any kind of military engagement and grew bored of the seemingly endless routines. He wanted to fight and on more than one occasion made his feelings known to Colonel Seacrest.

Seeing the whole picture and not limited by his own responsibilities, he realized the Army could make better use of Richard's skills. After seven months, he recommended Richard for transfer to an Army division stationed in England. He pushed through the required paperwork post haste. Grateful and relieved, Richard geared up for a transition from a cushy assignment to an exceedingly demanding one some 7,000 miles away. Shortly before Christmas, 1942, Richard received his orders and thanked Colonel Seacrest for believing in him. He hoped their paths would cross again. That didn't happen. Tragically, the colonel was killed while piloting a secret reconnaissance mission in the Pacific. Both engines in his B-25 Bomber malfunctioned. Unable to negotiate a safe water landing, the plane crashed and the crew of ten were killed instantly. When Richard learned about this event, he was very upset while also realizing had he stayed in Hawaii under Colonel Seacrest's command, he could have been on the airplane that went down.

Sitting in the back of two different airplanes on his way from Hickam to an airbase south of London, Richard read several articles in Stars and Stripes including an extensive piece on the Battle of Midway Island where the U.S. Navy earned a most important victory over the heretofore invincible Japanese Navy. Outsmarting and outmaneuvering experienced Japanese naval officers, the American leadership under U.S. Naval Fleet Admiral, Chester W. Nimitz, won the day. The victory changed the course of the war in the Pacific. Occurring just six months after the Japanese attack at Pearl Harbor, defense of Midway Atoll, a tiny point between the United States and Japan, was a critical air-sea battle. American dive bombers sunk four Japanese aircraft carriers and a heavy cruiser. "Hooray for the good guys," Richard shouted. "Let me at 'em." Tuns out, he would come face-to-face with a determined enemy in Europe, not in the Pacific.

Although 1942 proved to be a turning point of the war in Europe, the Allies anticipated heavy German resistance and soon became aware there were many battles yet to fight. The Wehrmacht and the SS Panzer Corps retreated as the Allies advanced but the Germans re-positioned for successful counter attacks, many of them in France. The German generals soon learned, however, the Americans possessed men, materials, and firepower equal to their own. The sheer number of U.S. soldiers, tanks, guns, and munitions engaged in combat was staggering. The harbinger of American might was voiced by Admiral Isorku Yamamoto following the successful attack on Pearl Harbor in 1941. While his naval subordinates celebrated too much and too soon in his opinion, he stated, "I am afraid we have awakened a sleeping giant." His prognostication was spot on.

When Richard arrived in England, he immediately called home to inquire about his mom. Now at home and resting comfortably, she was confined to her bed and in all likelihood would not begin rehabilitative services for some time. A volunteer, private duty nurse looked in on Janet daily, checked vital signs, and monitored her medications. She was a godsend and Ben provided monetary compensation when he could. Richard was somewhat encouraged and felt a bit better about her prognosis. But he was worried about her fragile state of mind exacerbated by the severity of the stroke she suffered. Ben James inquired about Richard's new assignment but understood that he couldn't provide many details. Richard asked him to share with Phyllis he was all right and promised to come home to her as soon as he could.

Phyllis had settled in to a regimen of work, exercise, and service as a volunteer at a USO center outside of town. Still worried but no longer in a depressed state, she accepted Richard's patriotic commitment, and at the same time was convinced of the inevitability of America winning the war and his safe return home. Life without her dear husband was difficult. She missed his voice, touch, and sense of humor. However, she and Lawrence Andersen — tall, handsome, and friendly - spent time together, making Richard's absence more palatable. Phyllis saw nothing wrong with talking to her new male friend and occasionally dating.

But her parents did not approve of their liaison. They understood she was lonely but a married woman's vows to her husband were sacrosanct. The family didn't discuss her connection and her parents avoided inquiring about her whereabouts on weekend evenings. Lawrence was totally smitten. After all, he found Phyllis' beauty, intelligence, and vitality irresistible. In some ways, she looked at Lawrence as a needed distraction; a short-term fix, if you will. Although he knew she was married and was doing her best to remain loyal to Richard, he couldn't help himself. Over time and not by design, sexual tension played out between the two. However, Phyllis remained strong and resisted.

Far away on the European continent, Richard immersed himself in training for a combat leadership role. Thoughts of his wife and the goings on at home were superseded by the prospects and responsibility of leading men into battle. For now, that's the way it had to be.

CHAPTER 17

Richard trained yet again for nearly a year alongside "Brits," as he called them, in several secret venues in both England and Scotland. His superior officers, both English and American, organized and monitored simulated war games and despite his lack of actual battle experience, he distinguished himself. Brave, focused, and a competent decision-maker, he befriended many fellow officers and enlisted men alike, earning their trust and respect. On several occasions, he laid down his weapon to come to the aid of an injured colleague, demonstrating his regard for their safety.

With nearly two years of training under his belt, Richard was more than ready for combat. Accordingly, he was sent to Italy in 1943, joining a seasoned British-American brigade in a forward position. He was second in command of a small infantry unit and observed enemy troop movements, radioed their positions, and didn't engage the enemy unless attacked. The second week of his new deployment, in the dark of night, he found himself in the middle of a fierce fusillade and watched bullets and other assorted incendiaries crisscross in the distance above him. A fiery red-light show, these fireworks were real and lethal.

His unit was soon attacked by a German patrol and hand-to-hand combat ensued near the town of Salerno. During this brief encounter, he killed several enemy soldiers, one by hand. In that encounter, his arm was sliced by a German Bolo knife. Undeterred, scared as hell, and bleeding badly, he kept fighting and, in the process, saved the life of an American sergeant. Seeing he was injured, the First Lieutenant in charge ordered him to the rear to have his arm looked at by a medic. After he was bandaged and medicated, Richard returned to the scene of the battle but by now the German patrol had disappeared into the night. His first encounter was both memorable and bloody. Due to his injury, Richard was awarded the Purple Heart in a brief ceremony a few weeks later, interrupted by shelling from German artillery some miles away. Also, unexpectedly, he was promoted to First Lieutenant due to his meritorious actions in battle. Richard learned that war had neither a heart or a soul and to always keep his head down. Basic training taught him well.

CHAPTER 18

On the other side of the globe Elbow Lake looked like a ghost town and was eerily quiet, particularly at night. Before the world was engulfed in war, the town bustled with commerce. No longer. Men of military age were either training in the United States or serving in some capacity overseas. Unemployment remained high and many shops closed with their owners moving to other cities. The citizenry nervously adapted to the conditions brought on by events in Europe and the Pacific. With the war on, resources such as iron, rubber, and steel were in short supply and there was not an abundance of food. Rationing of meat, butter, pork, and eggs made feeding families difficult and out of necessity, households were on strict budgets. Businesses carried on but most operated in the red. These were trying times.

Women in big cities working in aircraft and munitions factories were holding down the fort — working, housekeeping, raising children on their own, and through the USO sent supplies, foodstuffs, and well wishes to soldiers overseas. Life was

challenging and small towns like Elbow Lake struggled to stay above water. Although Ben James was
able to keep his auto repair shop open four days a
week, he was unable to pay his mortgage on a regular basis. Once again, however, his banker worked
with him — even reducing the monthly house note.
Michael Verducci was laid off by his insurance company due to insufficient customers. Few people
could afford to buy any type of insurance, but he
was resourceful and worked a full schedule clerking
at one of the town's grocery stories. Wife Cheryl
opened a private home laundry business, proving to
benefit many of the townspeople. She ironed for a
few friends at five cents per item. All in all, Elbow
Lake was 'making do.' Learning of United States'
military successes, they held on to the hope the war
would soon reach a conclusion, wanting so much
for their lives to return to normal. Unfortunately,
the war was far from over.

Lawrence worked at the local utility plant
and did very well for himself financially. Electricity,
gas, and water were living necessities and a small ca-
dre of workers, Lawrence included, provided service,
maintenance, and repair to Elbow Lake residents on
a regular basis. Due to his work background and
military training, he earned a decent living and had
the money to court Phyllis. Ten years her senior

and a Navy veteran, he found himself between a rock and a hard place. He was an empathetic, compassionate man and didn't want to be the source of division between Phyllis and Richard. Thus, he maintained a posture of acceptance, wishing Phyllis well, but nonetheless, developed a strong connection with her. He loved her. Phyllis liked spending time with him but her reticence about their relationship was understandable and she kept a safe distance. She, too, felt trapped emotionally and didn't want to completely alienate her parents. It was a no-win situation and she needed to talk it through with Lawrence.

On a bright, cold Saturday morning, Phyllis and Lawrence met for breakfast at an out-of-the-way cafe outside of town. Realizing townspeople and a few high school chums had seen them together, they were a topic of conversation. Phyllis was very concerned; embarrassed, really. Seen for years as one of the most popular and admired individuals in Elbow Lake, particularly for her efforts on behalf of the homeless, her image was tarnished. This hurt. In these times, the union of a man and a woman was considered sacred — binding, and forever. A relationship outside of marriage was a serious violation of societal mores. Thus, the two friends found themselves in deep water.

Phyllis and Lawrence sat face-to-face in a booth in the rear of the restaurant. They zipped up their jackets and sipped hot coffee before ordering food. Lawrence initiated the tête-à-tête and asked Phyllis how she was. "Not well. What are we doing, Lawrence? I am married and here I am cavorting with you while my husband is overseas in harm's way. I am humiliating myself and my parents, too."

"Yes, I know," Lawrence replied. "If you feel it best, perhaps we should stop seeing each other." Phyllis said that was the right thing to do.

While eating, the conversation shifted to Phyllis' mother-in-law. Phyllis shared she was improving steadily. Thanks to both physical and speech therapy, her mobility was enhanced and now spoke in words her husband and visitors understood. Phyllis was still employed at the gift shop and spent part of her weekends visiting with Janet. Ben was grateful.

During a recent visit, Phyllis said the two women talked primarily about Richard and although Phyllis had not received a letter in quite some time, she thought he was in England. "Mrs. James grasped my hand lovingly and told me I was Richard's rock. I felt consumed with guilt," Phyllis added. Lowering her head, she then looked up at Lawrence, frowned, and sighed. The couple finished their meal and agreed, sealed with a hug, to stop seeing each other, at least for the time being. Phyllis walked home and suddenly realized she would not continue to be victimized by her unhappiness. Bored, frustrated, lonely - missing Richard, she knew what she had to do.

CHAPTER 19

The Allied campaign in Italy and Sicily resulted in devastating loss of life — American, British, German, and Italian soldiers as well as civilians
killed or injured. The sheer numbers killed was in
the tens of thousands. Notwithstanding Italy's ca-
pitulation to the Allies in 1943 resulting in both a
military and political separation from Germany,
Hitler ordered his armies to fight on with or without the support of Italian soldiers and Benito Mus-
solini, the inept, unpopular leader. The Wehrmacht
and the SS infantry and tank divisions pressed
ahead, often assuming defensive positions and
fought hard to thwart the Allied push. Successful in
but a few skirmishes, their efforts failed. In order to
defend against Russian and American advances on
Germany proper, the majority of able-bodied soldiers retreated into the heartland.

Richard fought bravely and on at least two
occasions had close brushes with death. He applied
his extensive training and natural abilities in a variety of combat scenarios, many challenging and very
dangerous. Revered by the men serving with and
under him, he earned a well-deserved reputation as

an exceptional officer. Just when he got his bearings leading his men into battle, he was reassigned and sent back to England.

In multiple venues in and around London, thousands of men were assembling and preparing for an invasion of France. Richard joined them. Despite the intelligence gathered by German spies working in London, Operation Overlord was a well-kept secret. Under the direction of General Dwight D. Eisenhower, Supreme Allied Commander, the proposed invasion would consist of the most men, ships, and materials ever amassed in modern warfare. The precise date, time, and location of the initial assaults were known only to a few. The buzz among the troops was a constant, however, and most everyone knew something big was afoot. That scuttlebutt was more than a rumor; it was fact. Now armed and ready, the only thing standing in the way of the massive invasion was mother nature. Inclement weather compromised landing craft and air support for several days but finally, June 6, 1944, General Eisenhower ordered, "We go." The sight of an armada of hundreds of ships alerted the Germans that they were in for a hell of a fight. The long-anticipated D-Day had arrived.

First Lieutenant Richard James and his unit barely extricated themselves from the landing craft. The gate opened prematurely in deep water and the first three men out drowned and the next three were cut down. Richard went under water, but he managed to stay afloat while taking enemy fire. Nothing in his training had prepared him for what he now encountered. Head down, he ran to shore while fellow soldiers on either side of him were either killed or injured. Due to intense firepower from elevated positions above the beach, the Germans held a tremendous advantage.

Hundreds of Allied soldiers along most beachheads were killed before firing a shot, including members of Richard's unit. Their bloodied, limp bodies sprawled out, many face down in small depths of ocean water, painting a macabre, sickening picture. Those fortunate enough to make it to shore were soaking wet and due to the amount of water amassed in their lungs, vomited. Many passed out. All this occurred before any fired a shot. There was a heavy price paid in loss of life by Allied landing parties — American, British, and Canadian securing the beaches all along the coast.

Months in the making, the Germans had meticulously prepared for the Allied invasion. They constructed defensive fortifications all along France's southern coast — barb wire, mines, and nearly impenetrable, elevated concrete bunkers. Effective initially, their defenses kept the invasion force stalled temporarily but the enormity of Allied manpower, munitions, and resolve eventually prevailed. Although the beginning of the end for Nazi Germany, the trek to Berlin would be long, hard, and costly.

Two full days passed until Richard and his unit were able to forge a path up a nearly vertical hill that seemed like a mountain. Once on level ground, the officers who survived the landing reconnoitered and thanks to advanced intelligence provided by airmen in reconnaissance aircraft, the routes forward across France were established. However, knowing how and where to locate enemy troops was problematic. German resistance remained strong and their pill boxes with underground tunnels had to be destroyed one by one. Hand grenades, flame throwers, and automatic weapons did most of the damage. Observing enemy soldiers burned alive was a grotesque sight and the stench emanating from their burned bodies permeated the air. Allied soldiers covered their mouths with handkerchiefs and many became ill.

On the third night near a French village, a German patrol located Richard's unit. Apparently out of ammunition, they fixed bayonets and attacked with a vengeance. Hand-to-hand combat ensued and one of the unit's enlisted men, Michael Ray, was stabbed to death by two Germans, but Richard shot them both and they fell on his dead comrade. Ray's loss was heartbreaking.

There was a thin margin between life and death. War was a living hell, Richard thought, but he was doing all he could to defeat an enemy that seemed energized, well organized, and determined to win. Reports of deteriorating morale among the German ranks coupled with rumors of hundreds surrendering were highly exaggerated. They fought like wild men and none that Richard or his men encountered surrendered.

Camped out, resting, and recovering from the bloody conflict, a crow suddenly flew out of tall grass in the rear of the encampment screeching loudly, and the sleeping soldiers awoke, rifles cocked. "False alarm," said Richard. "It's just a bird." Awake now, the men stirred, yawning. Corporal Max Street offered his boss a cigarette and they quietly made small talk. Street confessed he was very frightened and missed his family. Richard expressed a similar sentiment. Neither men wanted to die.

"All we can do is our duty today," said the lieutenant. He added that tomorrow would take care of itself. Street nodded and fell silent. Meanwhile, the other soldiers perked up and opened their K-rations. Eating, often under duress, was not a regular occurrence. Avoiding death was. The entire group learned quickly that being on constant guard was necessary to survive. Small talk invariably referenced their platoon members massacred on the beach. They wondered who would take dog tags off the fallen and notify their superior officers and collectively agreed that had to be a terrible task.

Shortly before dawn, Richard was contacted by a radioman in a forward area directing him to proceed to a coordinate about five clicks north by northwest where a German machine gun nest was wreaking havoc on a depleted Army platoon that was pinned down with no place to go and running out of ammunition. Complying with the communication, Richard ordered his men to get up, move quickly, and follow him.

Walking slowly in a large pasture just as the sun was rising, Richard's unit came under heavy fire

from a tree line ahead. As shots rang out near their
position, the soldiers fell on their faces, crouched,
and dug their helmets in the ground. A Germany
sniper affixed high in a tree, surmising Richard was
the officer in charge, fired his weapon and hit the
lieutenant with three rounds, one puncturing his
left ear, the second grazing the front of his head,
and the last penetrating his right shoulder. Scream-
ing out in anguish, Richard fell backward and hit
his head on a rock. Blood spewed out from the af-
fected areas.

　　Corporal Mike Powers immediately wrapped
his head and shoulder in a towel — a makeshift
tourniquet, in an effort to contain the bleeding
from the wounds. Now in shock, Richard drifted
into a state of unconsciousness. Fortunately, a
medic from another unit appeared, administered to
the wounds as best he could, and injected morphine
into his arm to ease his pain. Meanwhile, the entire
unit of eight soldiers lie silent on the ground and
raised their heads only when the firing stopped.
One of Richard's most skilled marksmen, Private
Charles O'Ferris from West Virginia, eyeballed the
sniper hiding in a large tree through his rifle's tele-
scopic lens. One shot from O'Ferris' rifle shattered
the German's skull, and he fell a good distance to

the ground. The remainder of the German troops retreated into the woods.

The severity of Richard's injuries required a stretcher manned by two muscular medics who carried him to a triage location south of his unit's position. Although the surgeon was swamped treating injured soldiers, Richard's rank moved him to the front of the line. He examined the lieutenant and with the expert help of a seasoned surgical nurse, he operated on Richard's shoulder, stabilized and bandaged it after removing the bullet. However, Commander Benjamin L. McCoy, after treating and cleansing his face wound, believed it best to stitch up the damage to Richard's ear, the lobe dangling about but still attached. The extent of internal injury to his head could not be determined. First Lieutenant Richard James would never fight again.

CHAPTER 20

The Women's Army Corps (WAC) was the woman's branch of the United States Army and was converted to active duty status on July 1, 1943. Initially opposed by Congress, a concerned public echoed their view. However, a need existed to support the thousands of soldiers on active duty in the states and overseas. Enlist in the United States Army. Why not? That idea worked its way through Phyllis' mind on more than one occasion since she and Lawrence parted company. Boredom, a lack of purpose, and Richard's prolonged absence were adversely affecting her life.

Telling no one, she drove to a neighboring town to visit an Army recruitment office. When she walked in heads turned, understandably, but undeterred she sat down in the waiting area. A few minutes later, a broad-shouldered Army sergeant sporting a mustache and numerous medals on his chest greeted her and the two conversed. Although a typically chauvinistic alpha male, he was nice enough and very informative. Phyllis' questions were thoroughly addressed. He even lauded the wonderful things WAC women were doing and shared that General Douglas MacArthur, commander of the American Army in the Pacific theatre, stated WAC's were better soldiers than men — worked harder, seldom complained, and were willing to take orders without question. On the way home, she was now convinced that enlisting was the right thing to do. If serving was good enough for her husband, it was good enough for her. Although she was old enough to enlist without parental permission, she wanted their blessing but worried about their reaction to her plan.

The next day, Phyllis took the bull by the horns and spilled the beans. Much to her surprise, her parents thought enlisting a good idea and perhaps an antidote to her periodic bouts with depression. Mr. Verducci knew females were not permitted to engage in combat, only in administrative and support tasks. However, he wished to speak to the sergeant about his daughter's projected length of service and the various specialty options available for women. Turns out, the brightest and nimblest women recruits were trained as switchboard operators, many assigned to posts in England. Next came mechanics, and then bakers.

At week's end, Phyllis and her father met with the same sergeant and all of his questions were answered to his satisfaction. In the car driving home, Mr. Verducci said to Phyllis, "Your mother and I love you very much and believe your decision to enlist is wise. We just don't want you to get into harm's way."

Phyllis responded, "I am so lucky to have such wonderful parents."

After completing the necessary paperwork and passing her pre-induction physical, off Phyllis went to basic training in Iowa for an adventure of a lifetime. Not knowing that Richard had been injured in battle, her spirits were sky high as she waved good-bye to her parents at the train station. Even though it had been months since she had heard from him, somehow she knew he was alive.

CHAPTER 21

On June 14, 1944, Richard lurched forward, gasping, sweating. Startled and disoriented, he didn't know where he was. He looked about and realized he was in a hospital. On either side of his bed were standing barricades and his arm was connected to a needle. He tried to access memory - any memory - of what could have caused him to be in this strange place. An experienced nurse donning a white hat with a stethoscope around her neck walked up and stationed herself on the side of the bed next to his IV drip and inspected it. Nurse Kathleen McHale then offered a friendly greeting. "Hello lieutenant. How do you feel?"

Puzzled, Richard didn't comprehend the question and couldn't muster a reply. "Lieutenant?" The nurse placed a cup of water to his lips and manipulating a straw, he drank his fill. She examined his head bandage configuration as well as the wrap on his shoulder and said they looked fine. Smiling, she left the room and said she would be right back.

What the hell, Richard thought. Was this some sort of a dream? What had happened to him?

His nurse re-entered the room accompanied by two physicians wearing freshly-pressed lab coats. The tallest one, attending physician Dr. James Adams, sat down next to Richard and initiated a frank, one-way conversation. Richard leaned towards the doctor and paid close attention.

"Lieutenant, I will fill you in on what transpired on a field in France two weeks ago," he said. "On a patrol with your unit, you were shot three times by a sniper — one in the shoulder, another grazed your ear, and a third hit you on the front of your head. It is a miracle you survived. Your injuries were treated by an Army field surgeon who successfully operated on your shoulder and reattached your ear. He cleaned and bandaged your head. His actions saved your life. After you stabilized in a few days, you were flown to London and transported to this hospital. Are you with me so far?" Richard nodded out of respect but had no idea what the doctor was talking about.

"Since your arrival, you have gone in and out of consciousness, most likely due to tissue damage in your brain, and the nurses here have monitored you round-the- clock. Due to the bleeding in your brain, we haven't conducted tests to determine the extent of your head injury," he stated. Now it was the neurosurgeon's turn.

Dr. Raymond Spruance told Richard his head injury was localized in the temporal lobe of the brain which controls memory, among other vital functions. He asked if he had any recollection of the events on the battlefield described by Dr. Adams. Speaking for the first time, Richard said, "No."

Dr. Spruance tried to assure the lieutenant that in time his memory function would return to normal. That assertion was problematic and a bit optimistic since permanent memory loss was a possibility. The brain is a mysterious mechanism and sometimes operates in unpredictable ways. There was no way of knowing if Richard's long-term memory would function normally again.

Richard was tiring and overwhelmed by the information he received. Nurse McHale told Richard his wife and parents back home had been notified about his injury but not his specific location. "My wife?" Richard queried. He turned away and drifted off to sleep.

Meanwhile, thousands of miles away and having recently completed boot camp, Phyllis read a telegram from the War Department mailed to her by Richard's parents. She wept but was relieved he was alive.

Assignments for the WAC Corps, either stateside or overseas, were based on written tests, oral interviews, and physical agility. Phyllis' performance on the test batteries was exceptional. Accordingly, she was offered a slot in a pilot program. Titled Medical Assistant, this innovative program was established to provide much needed medical support on behalf of Army physicians, surgeons, nurses, and rehabilitation specialists to care for thousands of soldiers injured in battle. As luck would have it, the new program training venue was located in London, England, not far from the hospital where Richard was being treated. At the time, however, Phyllis was unaware of her husband's location or physical condition.

CHAPTER 22

Civilian personnel, chiefly females, worked in the War Department offices during the war in Washington D.C. and performed a variety of tasks including, but not limited to, tracking injured soldiers and notifying next of kin regarding their injuries and whereabouts. Many working 12-15 hour shifts due to the volume of injuries and deaths, responding to both telephone and wire communications from special Army units who provided names and dog tag numbers on injured, missing, and fallen troops, they logged each contact. The information they received was often limited because of security reasons. Due to the obvious dangers to which soldiers were exposed in battle, particularly in forward areas, and the constant movement of men and materials, word of the fate of each man from distant locations was often delayed much to the dismay of family members who agonized constantly about their loved one. But each man was afforded respect and the attention they deserved. Rightfully so.

Two units in the War Department concentrated on securing accurate information. One focused on the injured, and the other on men who

died in action. When a death was confirmed, a contingent of officers and clergy were notified stateside
in a location near the residence of the soldier. These
men had the unenviable task of driving to the
home and telling a family member the fate of their
father, brother, uncle, cousin, or nephew. This was
a thankless, sobering process and seldom did the
words offered on behalf of the deceased provide
comfort. The pain experienced by the family was
simply too great. Fortunately, Richard survived his
near-fatal injuries and seemed to be on the mend.

CHAPTER 23

Janet James was recovering from her stroke and demonstrating she could play a more independent role around the house caring for herself. She no longer needed a private duty nurse and self-medicated without a problem. Although she had months ahead to mend, she was well on her way. Knowing Richard was safe and hopefully receiving good care, wherever he was, put her mind at ease. But she had no idea he had suffered a brain injury as a result of being shot. Always the worry wart, the less she knew the better.

Labor Day weekend, 1944, Janet had a "coming out" party. Literally. She had not been outside once during the months of her confinement. She was a bit wobbly but managed to walk outside onto the front porch with help from her husband. "At last," she proclaimed, looking up at the sky and the surroundings. No more cabin fever. Ben helped her into the family vehicle and drove the short distance to the Verducci's where a low-key party was planned. The friends sat in the back yard and Cheryl served home-made chocolate cake and poured pink lemonade for the thirsty guests into tall glasses with ice. They exchanged small talk. Cheryl stated she couldn't believe Richard and Phyllis were both in the Army and somewhere overseas. Janet nodded but had no reply. It was just as well since everyone thought she might say something negative. But she was uncharacteristically silent. Janet was tired after a few hours of social time, so Ben thanked the Verducci's and drove her home.

Meanwhile, on the other side of town, Lawrence sat solemnly at the kitchen table, perplexed. He read a letter over and over and didn't know what to make of it. Was the sender asking or telling? He wasn't sure. Although he didn't want to get his hopes up, he felt somewhat optimistic. He then decided to take a long walk and think things over. No harm in that. He wanted so much to reconnect with her but knew it was only a remote possibility.

CHAPTER 24

A voyage across the Atlantic Ocean during war time was always a risk. But calm seas and a dearth of German U-Boat activity made for an uneventful excursion from New York to a seaport near London. Escorted by two United States destroyers, the hospital ship, Mercy, carried several tons of medical supplies, munitions, and a brigade of Army soldiers. A group of WACs including Private Phyllis James occupied a "women only" compartment on the lower deck. Having completed basic training, they all were headed to assignment somewhere in England and they seemed to enjoy the ocean breezes and free time aboard ship. Phyllis had no opportunity to experience those pleasures. Turns out, she was seasick most of the trip.

However, a fellow soldier, Private Shirley Kowal, extended herself day and night to care for her. The two become fast friends. She administered anti-seasick pills, kept Phyllis' fever down, and even provided a barf bucket. Phyllis lost nearly ten pounds during the three-week transatlantic voyage but felt much better when the shipped docked into port. Still unaware of Richard's precise location, her training at a camouflaged facility would soon begin. Phyllis learned her fellow soldiers had grown up in large and small cities, rural areas, and mountain regions. Tall, short, thin, portly, they all had one thing in common. They possessed an undying loyalty to America and committed to serve a two-year enlistment.

Approximately fifty in number, most were assigned as mechanics, bakers, or switchboard operators, the specialty areas sanctioned by the Army. A select group, however, Phyllis among them, qualified to train as medical assistants. Housed in barracks resembling Quonset huts, the women participated in a rigorous program, learning much in a short period of time. The Commanding Officers, Colonel Andrew Jones, a surgeon, and First Lieutenant Martha Reinhart, a nurse, conducted a no-nonsense, hands-on training focusing on the basics of diagnosis and treatment of minor and serious wounds — not as primary caregivers but in support of doctors and nurses. Jones and Reinhart had experienced triage care in rear areas on behalf of injured soldiers in Italy, France, and the Pacific.

A segment of the training involved displaying pictures of wounds and methods used for their treatment. Medical personnel, normally working in

a team, checked vital signs, administered appropri-
ate medications, bandaged and importantly, offered
reassuring words. The visuals were often grotesque
and made most of the trainees queasy. A few simply
weren't up to the blood and guts they would have
to confront and were assigned to another program.
The officers provided lessons - crash courses as it
were - Anatomy, Physiology, Kinesiology, Psychol-
ogy, Chemistry, and wound care. This provided a
framework for a general understanding of body and
mind functionality and healing, emphasizing all
means and measures to comfort injured soldiers. In
the case of minor injuries, the unspoken goal was to
get the soldiers back into battle as soon as possible.
The more seriously injured were often shipped
home or a regional hospital where they could receive more comprehensive treatment and rehabilitation. However, as fate would have it, Richard and
Phyllis were only miles apart.

CHAPTER 25

During the war from start to finish, there were thousands of injuries and deaths of American soldiers in both European and Pacific Theatres. The War Department, in conjunction with the various military services, established methods of communication to family members regarding the status of their loved one. This was an enormous task. Naturally, errors occurred and frequently inaccuracies were inadvertently communicated, mainly by telegraph, which caused anguish on the parts of families who were at the mercy of the wartime bureaucracies. But the agencies did their best and the personnel assigned to family notification were overwhelmed. Through no fault of their own, though, they became part of the problem.

Phyllis was the recipient of letters from her in-laws regarding Richard but was unable to keep track of where he was or the extent of his injuries. Consequently, she, her parents and Richard's parents were in the dark month after month regarding his condition and precise whereabouts. Never sure if no news was good news, they prayed often for his safe return. And with Phyllis overseas now, her safety was a concern, too.

CHAPTER 26

Richard's injuries were healing but his memory remained foggy. The neurologist monitored his condition and administered two cranial tests now that the bleeding in his brain had stopped. The tests revealed a fully functional short-term memory, validated by his recall of doctors' and nurses' names, the topics of conversations with them, and the types of meals he enjoyed. He especially liked the cafeteria meat loaf.

But his long-term memory was impaired. His caregivers, directed by Dr. Adams, decided not to converse with him about the extent of his injuries. Richard didn't fully understand what had happened and why he was hospitalized. There was no way of knowing if he would ever again recall past events of his life. It was obvious to all medical personnel treating him that he had to know he had been seriously injured. In the meantime, a most unusual, unforeseen event was about to take place.

CHAPTER 27

The war in Europe intensified in late 1944 and into the winter of 1945. The Allied armies pushed west into Belgium and Luxembourg, unwittingly assuming the Germans would offer token resistance. This was a gross misjudgment on the part of the Allied leadership. Hitler seized this opportunity to roll the dice, a risky but well-reasoned strategy in which he directed an all-out offensive. Veiled in secrecy, and in the snow and cold of the Ardennes forest, his armies launched a sustained and violent surprise attack that initially seemed destined to succeed. Known as the Battle of the Bulge, the Allies suffered mass casualties and retreated. The Germans seemed better acclimated to the freezing temperatures and they pressed on with no hesitation.

However, the Allies regrouped and launched a counterattack, eventually wearing down Hitler's men, most of whom were killed or captured. The price the Allies paid for their eventual victory was staggering. Over 20,000 American soldiers died, and all but one soldier in Richard's original unit suc-

cumbed. Due to determination, grit, and their ability to adapt, the Allies prevailed, and the German
army collapsed. The path now had been cleared to
move rapidly further west into Germany while at
the same time the Russians were marching ever
closer to Berlin from the east. Hitler and his grand
vision for a new world order lasting a thousand
years was doomed.

CHAPTER 28

Phyllis was performing well in her training, exhibiting exceptional proficiency on quizzes and practicums. Each day a different type of injury was discussed using a variety of visuals including actual combat photographs, many of which were gruesome. After providing details of the injuries, students were asked to offer treatment options. Interactions between the students and their superior officers were both frank and informative. Thankfully, each female benefited from learning about the various methods of wound treatment from their colonel and lieutenant, seasoned combat medical veterans.

In the evenings after returning from the mess hall, Phyllis closed the curtains around her bed and sat in a chair where she studied, wrote letters, and listened to news broadcasts on the radio. Word of steady Allied progress against Germany was encouraging. Of course, she thought constantly about Richard. She kept the lone letter he had sent months earlier along with other correspondence she received from her parents, in-laws, and special friends back home in a private, locked container.

A recent letter from Richard's father stated his son was very much alive, recovering in a London hospital from several battle-related injuries. He and other family members were not aware of the severity of his injuries. Hospitalized for nearly a month, Richard was feeling better and when he had the energy to travel, Dr. Adams planned to recommend he be allowed to go home.

Unbeknownst to Phyllis and her fellow trainees, a plan was in the works to visit a nearby London hospital. The purpose of this field exercise was to familiarize the females with policies and procedures utilized treating injured soldiers by conversing with the doctors and nurses who would share medical information from patient charts. London Memorial was a teaching hospital and daily rounds were conducted to bring medical staff up to speed on the status of injured soldiers.

Traveling by bus on a cloudy, rainy Friday morning, the WAC trainees arrived at 6 a.m. and ate breakfast in the hospital cafeteria. They whispered to each other that the food was much better here than what was served at their facility. Rounds, coordinated by Dr. Adams, were to begin precisely 7 a.m. on a medical surgical wing.

This event was to be a most bizarre experience for everyone. Soldiers with minor injuries, most of whom would be discharged in a day or two, observed the WAC contingent from their beds and shouted cat calls and a few whistles. One couldn't blame them as most had not seen or been in the company of a female for months. As the group walked down the hallway an orderly pushed Richard slowly in a wheelchair in the direction of the medical group walking toward them.

Suddenly, Phyllis saw him and screamed his name. Running now, she called out, "That is my husband." Stunned, silent — the entire group stopped in its tracks. As she moved closer, she said, "At last!" Richard stared at her and said nothing. He didn't recognize his wife. "Richard, it's me," and reached for him. He pulled away and his attendant shielded him from Phyllis who suddenly felt dizzy, fainted, and collapsed on the floor right in front of him.

Several individuals rushed to her including Nurse McHale who summoned an orderly. Placing her carefully on a gurney, she was moved her into a vacant room. One minute an observer and the next a patient, Phyllis was down for the count. She spent the night in the hospital for observation, but it was determined she was physically fine by morning. Her mental state was another matter. She was released and transported back to her training facility but not before she put up a fuss about seeing Richard. Denied access, Dr. Adams thought it best they not talk, at least for the time being. Phyllis agreed but wasn't happy about it. Why all the secrecy, she wondered.

CHAPTER 29

The incident in the hospital proved to be the tipping point. Dr. Adams, Dr. Spruance, Nurse McHale, Phyllis, her superior Colonel Jones, Richard and Psychologist Dr. Rita Cavandish, a civilian case worker who periodically consulted with medical teams in support of soldiers with brain injuries, all thought it best to have a meeting. Mercy Hospital CEO, Dr. Randolph Andersen, chaired. Phyllis was understandably confused about her husband's behavior and why the War Department or the Army failed to provide details about his health.

The atmosphere was thick from the outset but everyone was encouraged to put their cards on the table. Seated around a huge conference table on the first floor of the hospital, most of the invited participants were present and seated save Richard and Nurse McHale. After a few minutes of small talk, Richard entered the room with McHale holding his arm. The two took their seats across the table from Phyllis. This proved to be a very awkward moment and the contingent wondered how Richard and Phyllis would interact. They looked at each other, and Phyllis smiled. But Richard, as he had done the previous Friday, remained stoic. McHale sized up the two and thought she noticed a sparkle in Richard's eyes. Maybe. Maybe not.

Dr. Andersen made the introductions. Referencing his notes, he stated the purpose of the meeting was to update Richard's condition and to support him and his wife, Phyllis, any way possible. He then deferred to Dr. Adams who summarized Richard's medical history highlighting the injuries caused by German gunfire. He stated Richards's shoulder and ear damage had nearly healed but the extent of his head injury remained unknown. Dr. Spruance took it from there and provided a thorough analysis of the tests conducted to ascertain information about Richard's brain functionality. According to the neurosurgeon, as a result of taking a bullet in the head, his memory had been impaired and the prognosis for its reconstitution was uncertain. He then turned to Phyllis and asked her to speak.

Wearing the olive drab uniform, standard attire for WAC Army enlisted personnel, she took a deep breath and glanced at Richard. Her eyes were glassy and face a bit drawn, but she was composed. She said she loved Richard very much, with or without injuries, and that they had been childhood sweethearts. They married shortly before basic training and she hoped and prayed they would re-connect and fulfill their wedding vows.

Phyllis started to cry, and Colonel Jones comforted her. Phyllis stated, "I am disappointed. No. That's not it. I am angry I was not notified about the severity of my husband's head injury. After all, I am his wife and a soldier in the United States Army. I don't understand the reason for the breakdown in communication — not only to me, but to Richard's parents. Who can address this?"

Several of the group looked at each other and shrugged their shoulders. Phyllis lowered her head and stopped talking. While wiping her tears, Richard's countenance shifted noticeably. When Phyllis looked up, Richard smiled and extended his arm in her direction on the table. All the while, the psychologist took copious notes.

Everyone was concerned about Richard. That was a given. However, the feelings and frustration Phyllis expressed made the tone of the meeting very serious. Her words broke the ice and moving forward everyone looked for ways to reunite the couple. The immediate problem, though, despite Richard's positive body language on Phyllis' behalf, was that he didn't know her. The CEO called for a break at this point and a few made their way next door to the coffee room.

Next up was Dr. Cavandish, articulating her take on Richard's mental state. A tall, attractive brunette, wearing black-rimmed glasses, she was the youngest person in the room. Having interviewed Richard's doctors and Nurse McHale, examined his medical records, and briefly conversing with him, she affirmed his memory impairment seemed significant. "His short-term memory is in tack and despite the brain trauma, he otherwise appears healthy. The damaged area in his brain may heal over time." Dr. Spruance concurred.

Looking at Dr. Spruance, who Cavandish acknowledged was an exceptional surgeon, she said he did not recommend surgery. Doing so would be very dangerous and a mistake of any kind in the operating room could prove fatal. She went on to say that Richard and Phyllis would benefit from counseling and if his long-term memory was not restored, the couple could "start over." Marriage and divorce legalities aside, it was conceivable they could reconnect and grow back a viable, loving relationship. She cited instances of similar circumstances of couples with favorable outcomes.

"Mine is an optimistic assessment. In the meantime, Phyllis, you will need a boatload of patience and once he returns home, his parents will have to understand and accept he is starting a new life," she said. She concluded her remarks stating, without sounding juvenile, the married couple could rekindle their romance. They are both young and time was on their side. The group gave Dr. Cavandish nods of approval and Dr. Andersen commended her for the thoroughness of her assessment. The meeting was now adjourned, and Richard made his way to the door, but not before he glanced at Phyllis. She smiled and waved good-bye to him but was still upset the questions she posed at the outset of the meeting were not addressed. In fairness, however, none of the medical team present were responsible for communicating the status of injured soldiers. That was not within their purview.

CHAPTER 30

Richard's mind was spinning so much that he managed to block out the drone of the engines and the rattling of the supply containers. He was still confused regarding the circumstances resulting in his hospitalization and inability to remember people, places, and events. He was in a fog.

With a brief stopover in Greenland to refuel and accompanied by an Army medic reservist, both strapped in at the rear of the C-47 cargo plane, Richard was going home. It was January 3, 1945, and his lengthy hospitalization had ended. His parents waited nervously at an Army air base outside Minneapolis for the twenty-one-hour flight to arrive. They wondered how their son would greet them. Moreover, would he even recognize them?

CHAPTER 31

Two weeks earlier, the wheels were in motion for Richard's return home. After the meeting with the medical team, CEO Dr. Andersen phoned Richard's parents to provide current data about his condition and assured them he was recovering. Dr. Andersen pulled no punches and told them Richard's memory was impaired as a result of a bullet puncturing his brain. Needing further care once home, Richard was scheduled for treatment at a regional facility near Elbow Lake where counseling and rehabilitative services were to be provided on an outpatient basis. He also mentioned that their daughter-in-law had conversed with Richard, but that he didn't seem to recognize her.

The Army, normally sticklers for rules and procedures, considered the totality of the situation an extenuating circumstance and therefore recommended Phyllis be flown home after her training in London was completed. However, she was obligated to fulfill her enlistment and would be assigned to work at a civilian hospital somewhere in Minnesota. The Verducci's were thrilled their daughter would be home in a few months.

At the urging of the psychologist, Phyllis and Richard met face-to-face the day before he flew home in a small anteroom in the hospital basement. A tense encounter at first, Phyllis initiated the conversation, expressing her remorse about her husband's injuries, but grateful he was healing. His wife, she remained committed to him rain or shine.

Richard thanked her and stated, "I am sorry, I don't recognize you and don't remember getting married.

Phyllis explained, "We grew up in Elbow Lake, Minnesota, went to the same schools, and were childhood sweethearts. We married just before you left for Army basic training."

Richard shook his head. There was a pause in the conversation but in a few minutes, Richard stated he was going home the next day and that his parents were picking him up at the airport. Phyllis smiled and reached out to him.

At this point, Richard noticed her diamond wedding ring and said, "So, you are married."

Seizing this moment of spontaneous levity, she replied, "Yes, I am." Looking at the silver ring on his left hand, she expanded, "You must be married, too."

Richard responded, "I wish I knew." Both smiled.

Phyllis thought about their wedding and the vows they took, remembering vividly the words "in sickness and in health." They were so happy until the war separated them. She never expected she would ever have to fight to win back his heart. But fight she would. As Richard got up and made his way to the door, Phyllis considered giving him a hug — but resisted.

CHAPTER 32

The blatant lies and false promises propa-
gated by Nazi Propaganda Minister, Joseph Goebbels, couldn't save the Third Reich. In late spring,
1945, his words spoke of last-minute heroics and
new weapons that would win the war. The German
people had not seen the Fuhrer for months and an-
ticipating the worst, he isolated himself in his underground bunker in Berlin. His armies, what was
left of them, retreated in total disarray, squeezed by
Russian forces from the east and the Allies from the
west.

Thousands of German soldiers, bereft of
food, munitions, and competent leadership, surrendered to the Americans — knowing they would be
afforded humane treatment. Capture at the hands
of the Russians would be disastrous as legions of
the Wehrmacht and SS discovered. Russian soldiers
entering Berlin indiscriminately shot everyone in
sight including women, children, and the elderly.
Pregnant women in hospitals were raped and tor-
tured. The motivation for these atrocities stemmed
from Hitler's "scorched earth" tactics during both
their invasion of and retreat from Russia as they

burned villages, ravaged women, shot children, and killed livestock. It is estimated that over thirteen million Russian citizens were murdered or died of starvation.

In April 1945, Germany threw in the towel. Like rats running from a sinking ship, many of Hitler's henchmen fled as best they could. Most were captured. Those remaining loyal, including Joseph Goebbels, stayed on and took their own lives. Sadly, Goebbels poisoned his children and his wife. In an act of cowardice, Hitler shot himself and ordered his body burned. His wife, Eva Braun, succumbed by self-inflicted poison.

The few German generals still alive attempted to sue for peace with the Americans rather than the Russians, but this strategy failed. Believing that to the victors go the spoils, Joseph Stalin had every intention of procuring as much territory as possible and proved a crafty, if not deceitful negotiator dividing up Germany and other European nations. His goal of a communist-dominated Europe was real, and the beginnings of a cold war took root.

CHAPTER 33

Phyllis found it increasingly difficult to concentrate on the tasks and studies required of her training. Despite knowing Richard was home safe and that she was only weeks away from completing her assignment, she was blue. Soldier colleagues supported her and empathized, knowing she and Richard were estranged. To make matters worse, the weather in and around London was miserable. Extreme cold, winds, and seemingly daily downpours of rain were uncharacteristic for the spring, even by English standards.

The sun rarely made an appearance and when it did, it was short-lived. The Army supplied extra blankets, an abundance of outer and under garments, overcoats, caps, gloves, and socks but the freezing cold cut through all these accouterments. In addition, a contradiction puzzling the trainees was the plethora of electrical outlets in the barracks with no heaters anywhere to be found. Consequently, they often slept with their clothes on and many became ill. An absence of hot water made for short, cold showers.

After chow on a particularly cold evening, Phyllis read her deployment papers over and over and worried about the future. Was her marriage to Richard doomed? Would he ever regain his memory? The uncertainty of their lives moving forward was distressing and she felt she had no control. Then, suddenly, her mind wandered and thought about Lawrence. In a cruel, disloyal way she distanced herself from Richard for a moment, focusing on a man whose advances she had rejected. What was Lawrence doing now? She would find out once she got home.

CHAPTER 34

Meanwhile, across the Atlantic Ocean, Richard took a walk in his neighborhood trying to get his bearings. Home now for two weeks, he tried his best to recall his surroundings. However, he remained frustrated he was unable to do so. Ben and Janet James had welcomed him home with open arms and treated their son like a king. Occupying his old bedroom, newly painted and decorated by his mother, he was given free reign of the house. Eating delicious, home-cooked meals helped put back weight on his thin torso. Giving him space was essential in acclimating him to a new and very different life and neither parent pressed him for details about his experiences in the war. His father kept him busy during the day working at his auto repair shop. Richard was mechanically-inclined and seemed to enjoy the greasy tasks he performed, many of which took place under the cars he serviced.

Richard's parents mustered up all the patience and understanding of which they were capable. After all, he had suffered so much, physically and mentally and seemed lost in his own home.

Dealing with the effects of a brain injury was not easy and he wasn't the same young man who a few years earlier had the strength of a horse, the intellect of a scholar, and a winning personality. Richard didn't recognize his parents which deeply distressed them. Each day they hoped and prayed he would snap out of his funk, but any amount of wishing wouldn't make it happen.

One night after supper on his way to the bathroom, Ben noticed Richard sitting on his brother's bed. Looking in, Ben said, "This was your brother David's room."

Richard's reply was totally unexpected. "Yes, I know," he said softly with conviction.

Ben wasn't a doctor but thought his son's reply might mean he was having a breakthrough — even if it was a small one. Back in the kitchen where Janet was washing dishes, Ben shared their surprising verbal exchange. For the first time in a long while, Richard's mother smiled and hugged her husband. She had no words but shed plenty of tears.

CHAPTER 35

A letter arrived in the mail on a weekday while Ben and Richard were at work. Janet retrieved it out of the mailbox and was tempted to open it. The return address was the United States Army Headquarters, Washington D.C. When her men came home, she pointed to it on the entry way table and Richard looked at it. "Please open it, Richard," his mother admonished.

Moving to the living room and now seated, the Richard gave it to his father to read. The letter commended First Lieutenant Richard James for heroic and meritorious actions in battle on June 9, 1944, near a village in France against an aggressive enemy and while doing so sustained multiple gunshot injuries. It is with great pleasure and sincere gratitude the Army bestows on this brave soldier, the enclosed Purple Heart, his second. Further, the lieutenant is being recommended, pending congressional approval, for the Distinguished Service Cross. A grateful nation thanks you. Ben noted with the signature at the bottom — General George C. Marshall, United States Army Chief of Staff. Proud as any parents could be, Ben and Janet

beamed. Richard expressed no emotion, said nothing, and went to his room.

CHAPTER 36

Richard had been a well-liked, respected high school athlete with a high profile. Consequently, he was well known throughout the community. When he returned home, his neighbors, former classmates, and high school faculty wanted to greet him. Now, an injured former soldier, his parents thought it best to avoid such get- togethers as sharing the nature of his brain injury and the resulting loss of memory would create discomfort for visitors and Richard, too.

At the direction of the Army, Richard was receiving rehabilitative services including counseling from a private therapist, Dr. Ron Kurtz, an experienced, skilled mental health professional who met with Richard twice a week and conducted exercises designed to stimulate his temporal lobe, the organ in his brain controlling memory. Kurtz was pleasant, patient, and knowledgeable — a balding man in his late 50's who was careful not to push his patient too fast or too hard. He spoke with Richard's parents once a week on Fridays and provided updates on their son's progress or lack thereof. The latter was evident from the beginning and he agreed with Richard's doctors in England who believed the prognosis to retrieve his long-term memory was possible, but doubtful. Although his wife would soon be home to support him, the disconnect he was experiencing with the people in his life was real and to them, disconcerting.

Richard demonstrated an interest in Dr. Kurtz's receptionist, Nora, and they exchanged small talk while he waited to see the doctor. Having no trouble whatsoever expressing himself, he began to develop feelings for her, and asked if she wished to meet him for lunch prior to an afternoon session. Maintaining confidentiality and professional decorum, she declined. Thanking him for the invitation, she said perhaps they could meet sometime in the future. She was attracted to him, no doubt, but she wanted to keep her job. Eventually, Richard would become more persistent, wanting to socialize with this pretty young woman. Interestingly enough, he had not felt the same attraction to his own wife on the two occasions he and Phyllis met at the hospital in England.

CHAPTER 37

Victory in Europe (V-E Day) was wildly celebrated in many parts of the world with pronounced
and prolonged jubilation in America. Photographs
of servicemen kissing women in Times Square in
New York city appeared in hundreds of newspapers
throughout the country. The party was on.

Following nearly five years of conflict which
amounted to 68 months and over 2,000 days, Germany surrendered to an Allied delegation on May
7, 1945 in Reims, France. But all across beleaguered
Europe, the end was bittersweet. Visuals of bombed
cities, civilians carrying belongings running to who
knows where, and corpses plainly visible in streets,
country sides, and internment camps were images
difficult to stomach. For thousands of displaced
persons — emaciated, sick, helpless, and vulnerable
- the Allies provided relief and hope. The war's conclusion didn't come a minute too soon, but the af-
termath was horrific for thousands. American, British, Canadian, and Russian soldiers assigned to render life-saving assistance in the death camps were re-
pulsed. What would or could be done to acclimate
survivors to a new life? Sadly, many internees,

frightened and disoriented, refused food and medicine — precipitating their deaths.

Americans living in cities, big and small, including Elbow Lake, tracked the post-surrender events in newspapers and on radio broadcasts. They were relieved the war in Europe was over and lauded Hitler's demise. However, American soldiers were fighting in the Pacific against a fanatical Japanese Army. Kamikaze pilots wreaked havoc on American warships all along the Pacific corridor, sacrificing their lives at will with no hesitation to honor Emperor Hirohito. With many battles ahead, mostly on Japanese-occupied islands, the U.S. Navy and Marine Corps implemented an "island hopping" campaign ordered by Fleet Admiral Chester W. Nimitz. The objective was to cut off Japanese supply lines and move closer to mainland Japan. The number of casualties on both sides during these battles were incalculable. It became painfully obvious that Japanese civilians and homeland military forces were prepared to die to the last man, woman, and child. The other option was mass suicide. Either way, it was estimated a million Americans soldiers would suffer injury or death in the event an invasion of the Japanese mainland became necessary.

CHAPTER 38

The spur-of-the-moment getaway was just what the doctor ordered. Ben made a quick reservation for he and his wife, and the Verducci's at an isolated location high in the mountains near the Canadian border. Surrounded by greenery, pine trees, a stream running downhill outside the back door adjacent to a picture post card lake, the spacious cabin was an ideal place to relax. The serene location was the ticket for several days of conversation. Janet, not fully recovered from her stroke, was fatigued, and worried about Richard. Of course, the women would cook up a storm. A pleasure, not a chore, they both enjoyed. The husbands planned to fish.

Although the couples shared a mutual concern about Richard's mental state, they wondered whether Phyllis, once home, was up for the challenges of her husband's rehabilitation. Was their marriage on the rocks? Privately, Ben and Michael discussed the possibility of their union ending.

Ben and Michael arose at sun up on Saturday determined to catch lots of fish at the nearby lake.

Surprisingly, each man caught his limit in less than three hours. Their wives slept in and would be pleased to add fresh Walleye to the breakfast feast of eggs, pancakes, bacon, blueberry muffins, coffee and juice. Eating outside on a wooden table under a shade tree, the conversation was light; no mention was made of Richard or Phyllis. Janet was unusually chipper and, on this morning, looked younger than her age, thanks to a splash of make-up. The successful anglers devoured everything placed in front of them and couldn't help but brag about their fishing success. The women found their braggadocio humorous. However, they were glad to cook the large quantity of fish they managed to hook and prepared their catch for each meal that weekend.

The couples took a long walk in the afternoon but not too vigorous due to Janet's frail condition. Granted, she was feeling and looking better but due to a stroke, it wasn't advisable to overdo it. It was a three-hour drive to the nearest town having a hospital. Stopping periodically to drink from their thermos', the excursion was great exercise, but the high elevation had them all winded. When they returned, they spotted a big black bear off in the distance foraging for food. Taking no chances, the group stayed indoors for the afternoon and napped. As the sun disappeared into a gorgeous sunset, the temperature dropped significantly. Once awake, the men placed a few logs into the fireplace. Their wives wanted to enjoy a nice evening by the fire, bundled up with blankets, and drink hot chocolate. After dinner, they adjourned to the living room and did just that.

Unlike the casual chatter during their morning meal, the conversation on this evening was serious; actually, a bit heated at times. Questions posed had no definitive answers, only speculation and opinions. Back and forth, Janet was in motion seated on a creaky rocking chair positioned near the fireplace, a comforter covering her from head to toe. She didn't wait long to speak and when she did, there was an air of confidence and strength unlike the timid, whining behavior she had often displayed. Known to be reticent, even guarded, she directed her remarks to Ben and the Verducci's who were seated on a long, leather sectional in the living room directly across from her. She stated the obvious — a concern for her son's wellbeing. That was a given. She voiced concerns about his marriage to Phyllis, asking, "If Richard's recollection of people in his life, especially Phyllis, is permanently impaired, what is she to do?" Cheryl took it from there and did so forcefully.

"I think we may be getting ahead of ourselves. Phyllis isn't home yet, and we need to let things play out and not interfere with their relationship," she recommended.

The men nodded. Michael, although he agreed with his wife to an extent, said that the family will have to face the possibility that Richard and Phyllis might separate. That was a terrible thought, they agreed. Ben shared that the hospital CEO in London told him the psychologist attending the meeting with the medical team projected Richard and Phyllis might have to start their relationship over. She said the prospects of a happy outcome if they "dated" again were bleak, but not impossible. There was no way of knowing if the two would or could fall in love again. Ultimately, they might go their separate ways. The group talked late into the night and went to bed wondering if there was anything they could do to help their kids rekindle their relationship. Realistically, it was out of their control.

There wasn't much conversation during the drive home on Sunday. But they felt good about their weekend retreat and Janet suggested Ben reserve the cabin again for the holidays. She didn't say it but hoped and prayed the next visit to the mountains would include Richard and Phyllis. With only a few weeks until Phyllis came home, the fate of the couple was very much up in the air.

CHAPTER 39

Seated in the aisle on the front row of the airplane, when it rolled to a complete stop, Phyllis burst passed a shocked stewardess as the outer door opened, ran down the lengthy corridor, and made a bee line to her parents. There they were. Embracing, the trio laughed and cried simultaneously. This was a special moment. Her head up facing the huge glass windows, she saw the sun shining brightly. Her first words, "Finally, I had to travel thousands of miles to see the sun."

Michael carried Phyllis' suitcase behind the two women who walked hand in hand outside to the parking lot. Phyllis said, "I love you mom." They made small talk in the car for a bit until Phyllis fell asleep, exhausted. The length of the plane ride did her in and she needed rest. Barely able to undress when she got home, she crawled into her bed. She fell asleep without burrowing under the covers. Lights out.

Phyllis slept nearly 16 hours. When she got up, Cheryl fixed her a nice lunch and the two had a special time discussing this and that at the kitchen table. Michael, who still held a job clerking at a neighborhood grocery store, was working. After lunch Phyllis showered and put on makeup. She unpacked her suitcase and removed a large manila envelope. At first, she wanted to wait for her father to come home to open it, but she was too excited. So, she and her mother opened the contents in the living room.

The envelope contained important papers. Phyllis said the Army thought every piece of paper important. She pulled out verification of a ten day leave effective immediately, and assignment to a civilian hospital in Lake City, Minnesota, where she was to serve out the remainder of her enlistment — approximately ten months. This paper was to be signed by the hospital CEO on her last day of work and mailed to U.S. Army Headquarters in Washington D.C. where her formal discharge would be processed. Embossed with the Army gold seal, Colonel Andrew Jones commended Phyllis for her stellar work completing the medical assistant training and, upon approval of his commanding officer, promoted Phyllis to corporal. On a separate note, he recommended Corporal James consider applying to the WAC Officer Candidate School at the end of her enlistment. Looking through the documents, Cheryl told Phyllis how proud she was and gave her a hug. "When your father sees all these when he gets home, he will be happy and very proud," she stated. Phyllis said she was honored by the accolades given by Colonel Jones but had no intention of re-enlisting or applying to OCS. "I have to get my life back in order and save my marriage. These are my priorities right now, "she declared.

CHAPTER 40

Their lives had come full circle in a most un-expected way due to the outbreak of World War II. Living once again in their childhood homes only a few blocks apart, Richard and Phyllis settled in to a routine of work and little else. Several months after returning from overseas, Phyllis drove her father's car to work each week day morning —a distance of approximately 30 miles one-way. She enjoyed her experiences at Mt. Regal Hospital, a civilian facility, where she applied the skills acquired while training in London. She became adept at patient care, treating wounds and injuries, augmenting and assisting the work of highly skilled doctors and nurses. Phyllis became a staff favorite.

Richard, day by day, excelled in his mechanic tasks — reading books on automotive repair, conducting intricate tune-ups, and even learned to process accounts receivable. He continued to see Dr. Kurtz twice a week but by in large the sessions were not productive, at least as far as improving his memory was concerned. He didn't miss any appointments, late afternoon after work, due in part to conversing with Nora. She enjoyed the topics they discussed but politely rejected his advances, but it wasn't for lack of trying on Richard's part. Phyllis became increasingly frustrated because Richard ignored her and didn't answer phone calls. Although she had mixed feeling about seeing Lawrence again, they arranged informal "dates." Lawrence was all for it. However, Phyllis viewed their social encounters, all out of town in public venues as time fillers and made it clear theirs was a platonic relationship.

Dr. Kurtz shared Phyllis' frustration and was beginning to lose his patience with Richard, believing he wasn't taking their sessions seriously. Consequently, he thought it time to confront his recalcitrant patient. Although legally Dr. Kurtz didn't need permission, he phoned Richard and Phyllis' parents, telling them he was going to arrange a Saturday morning session. The James' and Verducci's didn't object; in fact, they thought his plan a good one and hoped for a positive outcome. Ben James didn't share his premonition with his wife, but privately believed a meeting with their son and daughter-in-law would be a waste of time. If Richard didn't want to try to reconnect, that was his choice and he would have to accept the consequences. His marriage lay in the balance and ending it would be heartbreaking.

Knowing words weren't necessarily a panacea resolving a complex relational issue, Dr. Kurtz had two objectives for the joint session. First, by asking questions and offering no judgments, he would get Richard and Phyllis talking to each other, hoping their interaction might fuel a possible resolution. Next, depending on the topics of their conversation, if things stalled and went south, he planned to confront Richard. Medically, he wasn't certain if Richard's memory remained impaired or if for some reason, he was "faking" it. If he now possessed the ability to recall heretofore unknown information, was he simply avoiding his wife? That was a burning question.

Initially, Richard and Phyllis spoke politely but soon Phyllis became agitated when her husband suddenly stopped talking and turned away from her. Then fireworks erupted when Dr. Kurtz quickly decided to abandon his plan. He had had enough. Forcefully and loudly, he said, "Richard, like it or not, this woman is your wife and deserves your complete attention and respect. If you can't remember her, I accept that, but you must reconcile with her or separate. I realize the viability of your marriage has changed dramatically due to your injuries, but if you have a desire to resurrect your relationship, then do it! Don't wait. You have the option of starting over and that might be a good thing. If not, you are both young and capable of finding another partner, but continuing this agony is futile. As my grandmother used to say, "Pee or get off the pot."

Richard was stunned. Phyllis said, "I couldn't have said it better myself. Thank you, Dr. Kurtz." She then got up, shook his hand, and gave Richard a menacing look before she left the room. As she walked to her car, her mind floated back to Lawrence. Maybe they were destined to be together after all.

Richard finally opened up and stripped away his stoic demeanor, a risk he had to take. Dr. Kurtz was all ears. "I am as frustrated as anybody about what a bullet has done to my life. Believe me when I say I truly don't have a recollection of a childhood with Phyllis, marrying her, and going off to war — even living in Elbow Lake. But, strangely, I remember my brother, David. He was a great kid and we shared many good times together. His death devastated me. Why he remains in my mind and heart is difficult to understand but he is there. Truthfully, Dr. Kurtz, I try not to think about the mess I am in and live day to day. Looking at the uniform hanging in my closet with purple hearts in the pocket gives me the creeps. Who was I a year ago? Where was I a year ago? Who am I now? The last thing I want is for Phyllis to be upset. Perhaps she would be better off letting me go."

Dr. Kurtz, pensive, listened carefully to every word Richard said and thanked him for sharing his innermost thoughts. He also apologized for being so direct, mercilessly so, but the harshness of his tone was necessary. Richard nodded his head and told him not to be so scary next time. Dr. Kurtz smiled and said O.K.

Before Richard left the office, he asked Dr. Kurtz what he would do if he were in his situation. His therapist replied, "Hell if I know. But eventually you have to do something. Stringing Phyllis along, intended or not, isn't fair. It's just not right. Let's discuss possible alternatives moving forward at our next session." Richard, releasing the excess emotion and stress burdening him for some time, broke down, and sobbed — a cathartic antidote to his pent-up feelings. He remained seated while Dr. Kurtz comforted him. This session was productive, if not electric, and appeared to be a good start resolving the dilemma Richard and Phyllis faced.

CHAPTER 41

Richard and Phyllis shared their version of the explosive counseling session with their parents immediately afterward. The Verducci's thought the directness displayed by Dr. Kurtz was both necessary and useful. However, since Phyllis left the office prior to Richard's conciliatory remarks, she and her family didn't see the entire picture. While they saw nothing but sadness and frustration from their daughter, they were not privy to the flood of emotions Richard was feeling and openly expressed.

Janet James was incensed, partly because Richard didn't share the entirety of the meeting's contents with her and Ben. He was too embarrassed to admit he let his guard down and had emoted openly for the first time since he had been home. Supportive of Richard in every way, her reaction was typically protective —a natural behavior for a mother who lost one son and held on tight to the other. Ben had a different take. He believed Richard was accountable for his mistreatment of Phyllis, regardless of his injury, and that refusing to socialize with her was unacceptable. He was pleased Dr. Kurtz dropped the hammer, but he was pessimistic about what their future would hold. From the mi-nute Richard enlisted in the Army to his injury in France to his stay at a hospital in England, he and his wife worried constantly. They were consumed by thoughts of their son to their own detriment. Like thousands of parents in the same boat concerned about a loved one overseas, they entered and re-mained in a depressed state and seldom did they ac-tually enjoy each other's company. Holidays and birthdays passed with little or no celebration. Janet was not demonstrably concerned about her own marital relationship — often rejecting Ben's at-tempts to converse or show affection. There was a dysfunctional paralysis between the two, mostly of Janet's doing.

CHAPTER 42

During the entire year of 1944, the fighting in the Pacific laid the groundwork for a final victory over Japan. Ferocious, bloody, and downright maniacal, battles on land and sea resulted in thousands of casualties, the majority Japanese. The U.S. offensive following the Gilbert and Marshall Islands campaign sought to destroy Japanese-held bases in the Pacific and support the Allied drive to retake the Philippines. Ultimately, defeating Japanese forces paved the way to construct bases for strategic bombing of mainland Japan.

Cloaked in secrecy during most of the war, scientists and engineers worked diligently on a revolutionary operation to create a weapon of mass destruction. Called the Manhattan Project, in the New Mexico desert and at other locations, experts conducted research and development to weaponize atomic bombs. High military officials, only a few in the know about the project, felt it necessary to have at their disposal powerful, highly destructive bombs for possible use against Japan. Whether or not such weapons could work was problematic.

Following the death of Franklin D. Roosevelt in April 1945, the new president, Harry S. Truman, was briefed on the goings on in New Mexico. Surprised he was not privy to information regarding the project, he did not seem at all reluctant to use the weapons if necessary. By July, the Japanese were reeling but kept fighting, committed to ultimate victory as plans for an all-out invasion of mainland Japan were being mapped. However, realizing massive American casualties was a strong possibility in the event of an American invasion, President Truman initiated a diplomatic end to the war, but Emperor Hirohito rejected peace proposals from American envoys. Then, not wanting to wait any longer, Truman gave the order.

Pilot Paul Tibbets' B-29, the Enola Gay, dropped the nearly five-ton atomic bomb on the Japanese city of Hiroshima on the morning of August 6, 1945. As a result, there were massive civilian casualties and the spread of radiation ensued, causing slow, painful deaths for thousands. Still resisting, the emperor refused to surrender. Consequently, a second atomic bomb was dropped three days later on Nagasaki, Japan. Soon thereafter, the emperor acquiesced.

The real mortality of the atomic bombs dropped on Japan will never be known. It is not unlikely that the estimates of killed and wounded in Hiroshima (150,000) and Nagasaki (75,000) are conservative numbers.

The signing of an unconditional surrender took place aboard the U.S.S. Missouri on September 2, 1945, in Tokyo Bay. Refereeing the event, American General Douglas MacArthur uttered these cold, final words, "These proceedings are closed." The end of the war in the Pacific had come but the cost in lives lost on both sides was astronomical.

CHAPTER 43

On October 1, 1945, Phyllis and three high school friends occupied a large booth at a popular Elbow Lake restaurant. Ellen, a short brunette, learned Phyllis was home and wanted to catch up. Accordingly, an all-girls' lunch was arranged. Phyllis' friends were anxious to learn about her and Richard and were all ears. Sara, a tall redhead, told Phyllis at the outset to spare no details, and she didn't disappoint.

Over soft drinks and hors d'oeuvres, Phyllis did most of the talking and quickly cut to the chase. She shared the circumstances of Richard's injuries, his hospitalization, her enlistment in the WAC's, their chance encounter in London, and the recent therapy session. The third friend, Barbara, a loquacious, perky blonde, tried to interrupt but the other girls wouldn't have it. "Go on, Phyllis," Ellen insisted.

Phyllis stated with a degree of alarm in her voice that her mind has been flooded with emotions, nearly all negative and worrisome, up and down like a rollercoaster. "Richard says he doesn't remember me, and I am at a loss of what to do."

When Phyllis paused, Ellen raised her hand like a kindergartener as the other two spoke at the same time. Phyllis looked at her and Ellen probed. "Are you thinking Richard is playing games with you or is his head injury calling the shots?"

Barbara expressed immediately she felt that was an odd question, but Phyllis answered. "Actually, that is a good question, perhaps the most important one of all. I just don't know. Since I have been home, he avoids me, won't talk on the phone or to me personally other than the one time in therapy. He is in a dark place and I don't know what to do." The waitress arrived to take their order and the talking stopped momentarily — cheeseburgers all around and refills on their drinks.

Barbara asked Phyllis if she wanted advice and Phyllis nodded her head. Ellen, Phyllis' best friend all through their school years, then popped a question that was shocking. "Have you been seeing someone else?

Phyllis' face turned beet red and said she was afraid someone would ask that. Truthfully, yes. He and I are just friends." The girls screeched loudly in unison and Phyllis asked them to quiet down. "We have dated a few times. No sex, just conversation. That is all, I promise you. Girl Scouts honor!"

Following a pause, everyone chatted about this and that to include what the single girls were doing with their lives. Ellen was going away to college soon, Sara was working at her father's drug store, and Barbara was in between jobs.

Although the group had been seated for over an hour, there was much more to discuss. After their plates were cleared, Phyllis asked what else the "busy bodies" wanted to know. "Well," said Ellen, "What else do you want to tell us, or better yet, are you seeking our advice?"

Phyllis stated, "I suppose I am." Then her friends went to the restroom and while there debated quickly what advice to offer. The question was, should Phyllis hang on as long as necessary with Richard? After all they had a history together and were still married. Or should she move on with her life? They hurriedly voted and walked quickly back to the table.

Phyllis, smiling, asked if they held a meeting in the restroom. Now the designated spokesperson, Ellen announced, "Yes, as a matter of fact we did, and it was unanimous. Get on with your life. We know you love Richard very much, but he isn't now the same man you married and will never be again."

Phyllis teared up and sighed. "Ellen, I think you might be right. I have a lot of thinking to do."

Sara then spoke up, "While you are thinking, let's order hot fudge sundaes." The group went into hysterics, laughed loudly, and heads turned in the restaurant.

Phyllis, trying to restore order, said, "Shhhh, you guys. Please calm down before we get kicked out of here." Three hours had passed and finally Phyllis said she had to leave. The meeting of the minds was over, but they planned another get-together for the following week. When everyone said their good-byes outside the restaurant, Phyllis' friends saluted her, mocking military protocol. Ellen said next time they wanted to hear about her WAC experiences and her job at the hospital. They embraced in a group hug and Phyllis walked to her car thinking simultaneously about Richard and Lawrence. Somehow, she felt more relaxed, thanks

to her school chums, but knew there were more
challenging times ahead.

CHAPTER 44

Michael and Cheryl Verducci sensed a Deja vu creeping back into the life of their daughter. When Richard left for basic training, Phyllis gradually fell into nearly a clinical depression and remained in that mode until her decision to enlist in the Army WAC. Training in the states and overseas elevated her spirits, giving her a sense of patriotic purpose. Focused and both physically and mentally stimulated, she concentrated on the many duties assigned, remaining understandably concerned about Richard's welfare. Home now, she was regressing once again into an unhealthy mindset, worried sick about Richard's brain injury and her marriage. Something had to be done, and soon.

Michael Verducci and Ben James had spoken privately about the possibility of a annulment or divorce and a local attorney came into the picture. Patrick Dowd, Harvard law school graduate, experienced litigator, and a local resident, provided the fathers with a free consultation. Phyllis gave the men the go-ahead to schedule a meeting. A man in his early 60's — tall, thin, and physically fit, he specialized in family law and divorce and was highly thought of in the Elbow Lake community. He addressed questions thoroughly and confidently. Taking the lead, Michael laid out the dilemma facing his daughter jeopardizing her marriage and inquired about legal options.

Dowd didn't need to research. He stated Richard's mental incapacity, when documented, served as legal grounds for annulment or divorce. He elaborated, "A judge will determine either or as the cause of a legal dissolution. Phyllis, an adult of legal age, must file for dissolution and Richard can contest it if he wishes. However, it is unlikely he, or his attorney if he employs one, could produce evidence negating her claim." Dowd said he would be happy to facilitate the process if Phyllis decided to move forward. Michael and Ben were satisfied with Dowd's legal acumen. Now it was up to Michael to discuss what he had learned with Phyllis and if she wanted to proceed. Ben would inform Richard. Ben knew his wife would hit the ceiling and she did.

Sitting side by side with Phyllis' on her bed, the Verducci's discussed the legalities offered by the attorney. Phyllis couldn't believe she was on the precipice of a monumental personal decision. As expected, her parents said they would support her whatever course of action she took. They wanted what was best but tried to remain neutral.

Later that evening, Phyllis phoned Ellen and explained the legal avenues for dissolution and that she was agonizing over the prospects of parting with Richard, the love of her life. Ellen offered no advice and listened. Phyllis thanked her for her friendship and support. They calendared another lunch, this time just the two of them.

A few blocks away, Richard closed his bedroom door, locked it, and opened the chest of drawers. He pulled out his wedding photo album from the top drawer, beneath his undergarments, and looked at pictures of he, Phyllis, and the wedding party. The faces looked somewhat familiar but other than Phyllis, he couldn't name them. He then opened an envelope containing his marriage license. His heart sank. Discouraged and confused, Richard wanted to reach out to his wife but was at a loss as to how, when, or where. After ruminating for a long time, he decided he would talk with Dr. Kurtz at their next session for his advice and counsel, hoping he wouldn't fly off the handle like he had done previously. That had been a horrible confrontation, but he knew Kurtz meant well. He placed the album and envelope back in the drawer and

within minutes fell asleep on the bed with all his
clothes on.

CHAPTER 45

The timing was odd. Japan's unconditional surrender was inked three weeks after the second atomic bomb was dropped. But the hospital administrator waited until late October to sponsor a party honoring all Americans who died in the war — in excess of 400,000. Gathered in a large assembly hall on the first floor, hospital personnel and a few special guests to including wives of deceased soldiers, listened to speeches given by local military officials and applauded politely. A number of American flags were affixed on the walls, tables were decorated with red, white, and blue papier Mache with insignias of all the military branches. A buffet spread provided more than enough food. The occasion of this event posed a strange contradiction, like celebrating Christmas in the summer. An orderly in the buffet line remarked sarcastically, "Why didn't the organizers wait until Halloween. We could have worn costumes."

A nurse standing in front of him said his comments were out of line and very disrespectful. She angrily addressed him, "You are a real smart-aleck." Phyllis, seated at a table near the dais, nodded her head in approval. Embarrassed, the orderly shuffled to the back of the line.

Phyllis had been working at Mt. Regal Hospital for nearly eight months, and due to a special arrangement was still employed by the United States Army. Accordingly, she wore black and gold scrubs and took orders from the chief hospital surgeon — assisting, as trained, caring for men wounded or seriously injured. Most were non-combatant civilians. She was proud to be a Nurse Assistant.

At the party, Phyllis socialized with hospital colleagues, one of whom was Dr. Norman Sinclair, a renowned Minnesota neurosurgeon. He learned Phyllis was on loan from the Army and inquired about why she was working in a civilian hospital. She offered an explanation, sharing her adventures in England and the nature of Richards's injuries — including his brain trauma. As one might expect, the doctor asked her to amplify. After all, treating such maladies was his specialty. Phyllis, now with the conversation more specific, asked about brain surgeries and Dr. Sinclair said they were high risk; success was problematic, occurring less than 10% of the time. Eschewing his professional advice, some patients insisted on surgery and, more often than not, died on the operating table. However, he said he would gladly facilitate an appointment to examine Richard if Phyllis provided his medical records. He smiled, gave her an impromptu hug, handed her his business card, and rushed off to see a patient.

Phyllis was cautiously optimistic. Dr. Sinclair was very knowledgeable and confident — a skilled, experienced neurosurgeon. She thought about sharing their encounter with her parents and in-laws but was reluctant. Friday, it was late and time to exit the party and drive home. On the way, Phyllis wondered if Richard would be willing to see Dr. Sinclair let alone provide his medical records. Further, she didn't know if intervening on Richard's behalf was a good idea in the first place. She felt badly that he continued to distance himself and in spite of his avoidance behavior, she kept hanging on — hoping he would want to rekindle a romance.

Realistically, however, that was just a dream. It seemed probable his brain injury would be a life-long health issue, precluding what she wanted most: a stable, loving marriage, children, a nice home, and, above all, happiness. Her friend Ellen was right; Richard wasn't the same man she married. Tears flowed down her face onto her top, so she pulled over to compose herself. After wiping the tears away, she sighed and thought that ending her marriage was something she dreaded. She was torn between life with him and without him.

CHAPTER 46

On Monday, Phyllis received a rare phone call at work. Her father-in-law said he had a growing concern about Richard and wanted to meet with her parents as soon as possible. Later that week in the evening, his wife out of town, Ben drove to the Verducci's where he shared what he considered important information about Richard. Among other things, Ben said Richard's actions were unusual of late. His son didn't want to socialize with anyone other than family, isolated himself in his room after dinner, stayed indoors — even on weekends, and often slept so soundly he had to be awakened by his mother or me in order to get up. Further, he stated, "My customers are beginning to complain about Richard. He takes too long to perform tune-ups and oil changes and, on several occasions, failed to replace bolts needing re-attachment to vehicle carburetors. These mistakes required return trips to the shop which I corrected them myself. While I did, Richard looked puzzled as if he didn't understand what he had one. My customers were understandably aggravated. I can't afford to lose their business."

Seated together on the couch facing Ben, Phyllis dropped her head and teared up. Michael Verducci didn't know what to say and neither did his wife. Ben had more to tell. He said he contacted Dr. Kurtz who stated he wasn't at all surprised.

Richard's behavior was consistent with brain trauma symptoms associated with the temporal lobe. He theorized the wiring in Richard's brain was malfunctioning and the cells in and around the injured area were, for lack of a better description, running amuck — trying to repair the damage. Dr. Kurtz said he was reading recent research studies about brain impairment and the frequencies of recovery were minimal and corrective surgeries rarely successful.

Phyllis spoke out regarding the recent conversation she had with Dr. Sinclair at the hospital who pretty much said the same thing about surgeries. But he offered to examine Richard if he was willing. Ben shook his head and stated emphatically Richard would object. Phyllis said, "Then what can we do?" No one had an answer.

CHAPTER 47

A loud knock on the front door awakened Ben James who was taking a late nap. Nearly 9 p.m., he got up and opened the door. The young man standing on the porch dressed in green Army fatigues introduced himself as Corporal Mike Powers. "I am sorry to bother you at this hour, sir, but does Lieutenant James live here?" A bit taken aback, Ben answered in the affirmative. Powers apologized again and said it had been quite an undertaking to find the correct address. Ben let him in and the corporal took a seat on the chair in the living room.

Ben surmised his son knew this soldier but reserved that suspicion for now. Powers asked how Richard was doing and said that he witnessed his injury in battle. Richard was his commanding officer. Ben hesitated to speak, and Powers recounted the circumstances of the bloody encounter with the Germans, providing specific details. He said he was the one who gave first aid and stopped the bleeding on the surface wounds. "I learned a few days later about the severity of Richard's head injury and that he was transported to a hospital in England. After that, I lost track of him and frankly, I was too busy killing Germans to give him much thought."

Ben smiled, relaxed and told Powers he was glad he stopped by. Ben noticed Powers' lips were parched white and went to the icebox for beer. They drank and talked past midnight. Ben explained Richard's head injury was serious and that his memory was impaired. Although undergoing rehab and therapy, he was not functioning like his old self, and everyone, including his wife, Phyllis, were very worried. Powers didn't know Phyllis was in the WAC and was surprised to learn she and Richard were living apart. Ben stated, "Theirs is a very unique situation, Mike. Richard has lost the ability to recall people and events, and still doesn't recognize Phyllis. His mother and I aren't sure he knows who we are. Very strange."

Corporal Powers sat back, sighed, and gulped down what was left of his third beer, shaking his head. "Unbelievable. I am very, very sorry Mr. James and will help Richard any way I can. I don't have family; none are living, so I am willing to move here," the soldier explained. Ben stood up and shook Powers' hand and then the two hugged.

Ending their time together, Ben said he didn't think Richard would recognize the man who saved his life. Handing Powers a piece of paper with his phone number, he asked him to call and expressed his appreciation for the visit. "Your coming here has been a blessing and I will tell my wife all about it. But I won't mention it to Richard just yet," he said.

Powers leaned forward before he opened the door and said Richard was a hell of a soldier and would die for his men. "We had great respect for your son," he finished. Ben went out on the porch teary-eyed and waved good-bye.

CHAPTER 48

World War II was the largest and costliest war in human history. After victory had been won in Europe and the Pacific there remained a Herculean task bringing home the thousands of military personnel scattered across the globe. Corporal Mike Powers was one of the lucky ones to catch a large cargo transport in late 1945, eventually docking in New York harbor. He was the only survivor of Richard's platoon. His comrades were afforded temporary graves until they were buried at a large cemetery in Normandy.

Operation Magic Carpet repatriated G.I.'s and in doing so required nearly as much planning as many of the battles of the preceding war years. Powers' good fortune continued as many of his countrymen - truck and taxi drivers, extended themselves by transporting him and others to their homes, some distances of over 2,000 miles, and only charged for their gasoline. These patriotic acts of kindness were commonplace.

In December 1945, at the onset of the operation, almost 8 million Allied troops waited to begin their journeys home. During the 14 months of the operation, an average of 435,000 military personnel were transported back every month. The record for a single ship was set by an aircraft carrier, the U.S.S. Saratoga, which repatriated nearly 30,000 soldiers. The operation also involved returning German and Italian POW's to Europe, a complicated task at best.

In September 1945, the Pacific phase of the operation began to bring back those stationed in Southeast Asia and territories of the Pacific Ocean. The total, approximately 370 vessels amassed included carriers, battleships, and destroyers. Even luxury passenger ships, the Queen Elizabeth and the Queen Mary, were drafted into service. There were two million soldiers eligible to be relieved of active duty waiting to be returned home in time to spend Christmas with their families (sometimes referred to as Operation Santa Claus). These voyages were often difficult, hindered by heavy storms. The password for every soldier going home was patience.

CHAPTER 49

Over lunch, Phyllis and Ellen discussed the decision Phyllis knew she had to make. Living in limbo was unbearably frustrating. Her momentous choice was not like picking a color for a new car. It was life-altering. On this occasion, Ellen once again didn't offer an opinion, just her undying support and friendship. She wondered what she would do in a similar circumstance although the situation confronting Phyllis was highly unusual. Phyllis was still in love with Richard but letting him go seemed to be the right thing to do. After an hour of give and take, Phyllis ended the encounter, telling Ellen she had made a decision and planned to meet with attorney Patrick Dowd to begin the necessary paperwork to dissolve her marriage. Both women broke down and sobbed.

Phyllis waited a few days and shared the decision with her parents. They were saddened but agreed it was for the best. Phyllis said, "I will meet with Richard's parents and explain the reasoning behind my decision. Simply put, he doesn't know me, avoids communicating, and it is painfully obvious he is not interested in developing a romantic relationship. I am willing to start over but apparently, he isn't. His father will understand but Mrs. James, his protector and advocate, will blame me." Michael Verducci asked if Phyllis wanted him to accompany her when she met with Richard's parents. Uncomfortable, awkward, and emotional as it might be, Phyllis would go it alone.

CHAPTER 50

Phyllis needed to get away. What played out in the judge's chambers and her encounter with Lawrence afterwards weighed heavily on her mind. She had accrued vacation time at the hospital, so she and Ellen decided to take a road trip somewhere, anywhere. On a dry, warm Saturday morning Ellen drove up to the curb in front of the Verducci's house in a rented, red Chevrolet convertible, honked the horn, scooped up Phyllis, and off they went. Since the trip was spur-of-the-moment, they didn't make a hotel reservation but neither woman seemed to care. Ellen immediately put the top down and Phyllis' hair blew freely as did Ellen's. Once they reached the expressway, Ellen asked Phyllis which way to go — north or south. Phyllis responded, "You pick, I don't care." Ellen nodded and drove south towards Wisconsin.

The radio turned to maximum volume, the two friends exchanged small talk but could barely hear each other. There was little traffic and Ellen motored along, careful not to exceed the speed limit. Two hours into their drive, Ellen spotted a cafe to the right of the expressway, pulled over and parked. Phyllis jumped out and headed straight to the restroom while Ellen sat in an empty booth in the back of the restaurant. Both were famished, and they ordered the same thing — pancakes, sausage, and coffee. They devoured their food quickly and without uttering a word. Once finished, however, they had a somber conversation.

Ellen initiated. "What did Richard's mother have to say when you told her you were going to petition to dissolve the marriage?"

Phyllis responded, "Actually, I was quite surprised. She took the news well but cried. Richard's father knew what I planned to say and was very understanding. They really are nice people."

Ellen then questioned Phyllis about the court proceeding. "Will Richard contest your petition?" Phyllis paused and said she wasn't sure what Richard or his attorney would do. "It's out of my hands. It will be up to the judge."

Later that day after crossing the state line into Wisconsin, Phyllis, now driving, noticed a motel and pulled over. The women registered for one night. The seven-hour drive was refreshing but they were fatigued and ready to call it a day. Before they

bedded down, however, they looked at a road map
and a list of events they had picked up at the front
desk. Phyllis, now in her nightgown, was pleased
that they weren't far from West Allis, Wisconsin,
where the state fair was taking place. Tomorrow was
the last day and she thought attending would be
fun. Ellen agreed. Before lights out, Phyllis called
her mother and told her she and Ellen were safe
and would be home late Monday.

CHAPTER 51

The Wisconsin State Fair was located in a suburb of Milwaukee near several sprawling cheese farms. The fair organizes spared no expense or effort and few people knew what a huge task it was to put everything together. A hundred or so volunteers, mostly teenagers, helped out. The last day of this popular, annual event was spectacular —a mixture of sights, sounds, colors, and activities with enormous amounts of food. Music blasted from large speakers positioned throughout the ten-acre venue during the day. At night after 6 p.m., several bands played live music including hit tunes from famous bandleaders Glenn Miller, Tommy Dorsey, and Benny Goodman. With plenty of floor space in an enclosed mini-bandstand, adults danced until they dropped.

Phyllis and Ellen stopped in their tracks upon entering to take it all in. Booths decorated in red, white, and blue commemorating America's recent victory in World War II proffered games for young and old while vendors sold hot dogs on a stick, cotton candy, snow cones, corn on the cob, pretzels, soda pop, and beer. A popular victual was the white or yellow cheese balls. The mood was festive.

In the distance a Ferris wheel, large roller-coaster, shooting galleries, dunk tank, and livestock exhibits could be seen. Callers walking to and fro directed the crowds to enclosures where a variety of clothing, jewelry, ceramics, and accessories were available for purchase. Skits in quaint outside arenas acted by local high school drama students were of particular interest to children, many of whom ran amok throughout the grounds. The friends enjoyed every minute and purchased beads they wore around their necks, affixed fake flowers to their hair, and won stuffed animals at the basketball hoop toss. They rode the merry-go-round, walked miles and ate too much, necessitating stopping to talk and recharge their batteries at rest areas.

Earlier in the day, they visited several livestock exhibits. Born on a farm in southern Minnesota, Ellen loved animals of all kinds and spotted a pen filled with piglets — all for sale. She couldn't help herself and despite Phyllis' objection, bought an adorable baby gilt — a female pig. Attempting to convince Phyllis of their worth, she stated, "Pigs are intelligent and easy to train." Phyllis rolled her eyes. The pair would return before the fair closed at 11 p.m. and pick up Ellen's new pet, who waited in a bright pink carrier.

Pitch dark, the drive home was immediately interrupted. Ellen was startled to see an animal on the road ahead, braked, swerved to the right, and careened down an embankment. Both women screamed. All at once, Phyllis' passenger door opened wide and as the vehicle was not equipped with seatbelts, she was thrown to the ground and rolled over writhing in pain. Ellen adeptly maneuvered the vehicle and stopped, somehow keeping it upright. She was unhurt, and the piglet seemed unfazed in the back seat.

A good Samaritan stopped her pick-up truck, pulled over, got out, and walked carefully down the depression to render assistance. As luck would have it, a state trooper also witnessed the accident and immediately radioed for an ambulance and an emergency vehicle. He joined the good Samaritan and Ellen, administering first aid to Phyllis, now barely conscious. Ellen bent down, stroked Phyllis' head to comfort her friend. She thought it seemed like an eternity until the ambulance arrived. In about 20 minutes, two burly men made their way down the hill with a stretcher and carried Phyllis to their vehicle. Ellen and her new pet accompanied

Phyllis in the ambulance to a Milwaukee hospital, not far down the road. Ellen thanked the woman and state trooper for their help.

Placed on a gurney in a receiving room, the emergency room physician, assisted by two nurses, examined Phyllis, checked her vital signs, and administered medication to alleviate her pain. Stabilized in a few minutes, she was bruised, particularly in her upper body. Later, X-rays revealed a broken right arm and a punctured lung. The physician explained the extent of Phyllis' injuries to Ellen in the lobby and said she would recover in no time. Silently, Ellen thought his assessment was a bit premature but hoped he was right. Ellen used a pay phone in the lobby and called Phyllis' parents and hers. Asleep when called, the Verducci's quickly dressed and drove to the hospital post haste, a distance of some 300 miles. The ambulance attendants brought the squealing pig into the lobby and placed the carrier near Ellen's purse. A pig in a hospital was an odd sight and several people, including the admitting nurse, stared at it. The pig squealed back, sensing their disapproval.

Phyllis was admitted to the hospital and occupied a room on the third floor. Medicated heavily, she slept nearly ten hours. Ellen was exhausted and slept in an uncomfortable chair next to the bed. Phyllis survived a potentially fatal accident and was very fortunate to have avoided serious injury.

CHAPTER 52

Several days later, Phyllis was home resting. She made it clear to her parents she didn't like the plaster of Paris cast on her arm which extended from the wrist to her shoulder. She said it was too tight and itched, but her mother tried to convince her that the cast would heal the broken bone faster than a sling. Ellen felt badly about Phyllis' injury and blamed herself. She visited her every day and brought flowers.

At Phyllis' request, Ellen left the pig in her car. Phyllis would be out of commission for at least a month and out of work. Her supervisor was very kind and sympathetic, telling her in a phone conversation to take all the time she needed. Phyllis didn't suffer a loss of appetite and ate everything her mother prepared, and then some. When she wasn't foraging for food, she slept morning, noon, and night and complained constantly about the cast.

CHAPTER 53

Weeks into her recovery, Phyllis' mother told her Richard had called and said he wanted to visit. Phyllis was shocked and initially had mixed emotions about a visit. But Richard persisted with telephone calls to check on her and asked permission to stop by. Finally, Phyllis gave in.

Feeling better now, she put on makeup, brushed her hair, and applied red lipstick. Cheryl let Richard in and the behavior he exhibited was in stark contrast to that he had previously displayed. Once in the living room, Richard sat in a big chair, Phyllis on the sofa clutching the bear she won at the fair. She noticed immediately the change in his demeanor. He was friendly, polite, and said how sorry he was about the accident. He didn't come right out to ask her to withdraw the petition to dissolve their marriage, but it was obvious he wanted something from her. Phyllis couldn't believe he was in the house after ignoring and avoiding her for months on end. Why the change, she wondered?

After a short and somewhat awkward conversation, Phyllis said, "Richard, I am tired."

He got up quickly and replied, "Of course. Feel better." He shook her left hand, smiled, and said he hoped to see her again soon.

As soon as he closed the front door, Phyllis' mother rushed into the living room and asked what Richard had said. "Mom, you were spying and heard every word," Phyllis proclaimed.

She confessed sheepishly and asked, "What now?"

"Good question, mother. I still love him, but I don't think I want a life with him. Ever since his injury, my existence has been turned upside down. Being married to a stranger has been weird and I don't feel good about it." Cheryl Verducci nodded her head. Phyllis got up and walked into her bedroom, opened the top dresser drawer, and pulled out her wedding pictures. Viewing them brought back good memories. But moving forward, she knew she had to take control of her future with or without Richard.

CHAPTER 54

Colleagues at the hospital welcomed Phyllis back with open arms. She gladly accepted hugs from the women on her medical-surgical floor. Absent from the job she loved for too long, she soon settled in to a normal routine. She rejoiced the previous week at her doctor's office where a medical technician removed her cast. Heavy, it took an electric saw to cut it off. That evening, her parents took her out for dinner celebrating good-bye to the monster cast. "Good riddance," Phyllis shouted, lifting a glass brimming with red wine. Three wine glasses touching lightly, it was a happy toast.

The clerk at Judge Strasser's office contacted Phyllis to reschedule the final hearing on her petition and she agreed to calendar a date two weeks hence. Although Richard had apparently decided not to contest her petition, he was trying to reconnect with her to no avail. Phyllis held special memories of their years and times together and reserved a place in her heart for him. That would be a constant. Unfortunately, his injury turned him into a different man and Phyllis believed he couldn't provide the life she wanted. Tired of constant drama, angst, frustration, and sleepless nights, she wanted her life to move in a different direction. Despite recent efforts on his part, Richard remained a wild card. Too little, too late, she thought. Their marriage couldn't be saved. That ship had sailed.

Phyllis was ready to make major changes in her life. In six months, her enlistment with the Army would expire and she wasn't sure she wanted to continue working at the hospital. In the local paper, a doctor's office in Elbow Lake advertised an opening for a nurse that prompted interest. This employment opportunity was promising and, if hired, precluded the daily commute to the hospital. In addition, Ellen made it known she was seeking a roommate to help defray her rent payment. Phyllis insisted she be put at the top of the list. Rooming with Ellen had advantages. The friends were two peas in a pod. Besides, Ellen continued to be a wonderful support through thick and thin. Phyllis wanted to move out of her parents' house, feeling she had worn out her welcome. That was a miscalculation as her parents loved having her around. However, Phyllis believed it was time to shed her dependence on them.

CHAPTER 55

Michael and Cheryl Verducci, Phyllis, and Ellen sat around the dining room table a few hours
after the hearing. As expected, the judge approved
Phyllis' petition with no objection from Richard's
attorney. Strangely enough, Richard did not attend.
A cold, dark day, the group talked quietly. There
was no cause to celebrate, just relief. Ellen put her
arm around Phyllis who seemed slightly shaken by
the finality of the event. Clutching the paperwork
signed by the judge, she looked down and sipped a
cup of coffee. No one knew what to say. Phyllis was
upset about Richards's absence from the hearing
and wondered what he might have said to her had
he attended. Her father, for the moment out of
character, stated firmly, "At some level, I feel sorry
for Richard. He fought for his country and paid a
heavy price. But he lacked the fortitude to confront
the reality he lost a precious woman and the chance
to rebuild with her."

Chuckling, "Speaking in the third person
just isn't your style, but thank you, father, "Phyllis
said. "That terrible war changed the lives of thou-

sands and the deaths of millions. Richard was a victim. Not fair. He is a good man, but he lost his way," she lamented.

CHAPTER 56

On Christmas Eve, 1945 Richard and his parents experienced an unusually solemn celebration, more like a wake. A tree with few decorations stood in the living room with no presents underneath. Janet, sitting like a ghost on the sofa, couldn't muster a smile while her husband forced one. Once again, an occasion meant to be festive was filled with doom and gloom. Richard sat in a chair and when carolers knocked on the door, he got up, went to the window near the front door and waved them off. When Ben tried to play Christmas music on their phonograph, Janet ran into her bedroom, sulking. Phyllis' petition ending the marriage to Richard had devastated her, but Ben believed it was something everyone had to accept. Richard didn't blame Phyllis. She deserved better.

On the other side of town, Phyllis, her parents, Ellen, and Lawrence celebrated in earnest at the Verducci home. Colored lights affixed throughout the huge fir tree twinkled, large bulbs hung in front and rear, and everyone hung tensel carefully, one strand at a time. That was a procedure Phyllis insisted on ever since she was a child. Michael Verducci did the honors, per family tradition, placing a large white star on the top of the tree. Quite unexpectedly, Lawrence played Christmas tunes on the piano and received accolades highlighted by a kiss from Phyllis. He played from memory — no sheet music. Cheryl prepared a delectable spread — veggies, ham, potato salad, deviled eggs, and pickles while her husband put out a large punchbowl full of lime sherbet drowning in champagne, his own recipe. The chocolate cake dessert baked in the oven to be served later that evening.

Gifts were exchanged after midnight, also a Verducci holiday custom. With everyone seated, Lawrence called attention to a tiny box under the tree and asked Phyllis to open it. She blushed and thought she knew the contents. On her knees, she peeled off the ribbon and wrapping paper and pulled out a gorgeous ring with a purple stone. A chorus of ooh's and aah's followed from the group. Phyllis gawked at it for an extended moment, placed it on her finger, and gave Lawrence a big hug before placing it back in the box.

Cheryl said, "Is that what I think it is?"

"No mam, it's just a special present for your daughter," Lawrence replied.

Phyllis and Ellen walked arm in arm into the kitchen to check on the cake where Ellen said, "I thought it was an engagement ring."

"No, silly, he wouldn't give me an engagement ring in front of my family," Phyllis exclaimed. Besides, he has to ask me first and get my father's permission. He knows the drill."

Suddenly Ellen's pig escaped from her carrier in the bedroom and squealed like there was no tomorrow. Everyone laughed heartily. This was the first time in years Phyllis felt truly happy. She gave no thought to Richard.

CHAPTER 57

Officially she was now Ellen's new roommate and it didn't take long to box up Phyllis' belongings from her parents' house. Typically female, she had oodles of clothes. When taking them out of the closet, her wedding dress was at the far end, covered by plastic. Ellen, always the inquisitive one, asked, "What are you going to do with your dress?"

Phyllis paused, shook her head, "I honestly don't know but you can wear it at your wedding if you wish — that is if you don't gain a lot of weight before then." Ellen laughed.

Mrs. Verducci hovered, attempting to help and suddenly started to cry. Phyllis stopped what she was doing and said, "It's O.K. mom. Everything will be all right."

Wiping her nose with a tissue, she remembered a letter that came in the mail earlier in the week and handed it to Phyllis. "What's this?" Phyllis asked. Her mom said it appeared to be a letter from Richard. Phyllis took the letter and placed it in her purse. A minor miracle, Phyllis' things fit in

Ellen's car. Now on the parkway, the Verducci's hugged their daughter and thanked Ellen for being such a good friend. They waved good-bye.

On the road a few minutes, Phyllis barked out a most sarcastic remark to Ellen. "Try not to run over an animal this time." Ellen got the joke and said, "ha, ha." She then asked Phyllis if she was going to open Richard's letter. Phyllis responded in a quiet voice, "No, Ellen. I just can't."

That evening at Ellen's apartment, the friends talked, polished off two bottles of wine, and talked some more. Ellen had to bite her tongue and didn't further inquire about the letter. At nearly two in the morning, Ellen ushered Phyllis into the guest room, her new digs. Small but freshly cleaned and smartly decorated, it was neat and tidy. Ellen had purchased new, fluffy curtains for the window and a checkered bedspread. The sheets were crispy and the two pillows were as soft as silk.

Phyllis remarked happily, "Is this space for me or a queen?"

Ellen bowed and said, "It's just right for you, Your Majesty." Phyllis offered sincere thanks for her friendship, sealed with a hug. Ellen bowed

again, welcomed Phyllis to her new home, said
goodnight, and closed the bedroom door behind
her.

Phyllis was very tired. She put on a flannel
nightgown, brushed her teeth in the adjoining bathroom, and slipped under the covers. Turning
around, she opened the window behind the bed. It
was a clear night, and she looked at the stars and
gazed at the Milky Way. Before she turned out the
light on the nightstand, she said a prayer and then
glanced at Richard's letter propped up on the
dresser. She couldn't help wondering what he had
written but she would never read it.

CHAPTER 58

The deadly bullet penetrating First Lieutenant Richard James skull altered his future and that
of his family. All-American athlete - intelligent,
handsome, humble, cherished son and husband - he
earned the respect and admiration of all who knew
him. Endeared by soldiers under his command, his
leadership and affable nature inspired them. As fate
would have it, however, his life and health were se-
verely impacted by an enemy against whom he
fought valiantly.

Richard and Phyllis, childhood sweethearts,
early on seemed destined to live a long, happy life
together. But it wasn't to be. Richard's patriotic fervor exemplified love for his country and winning
the war was his highest personal and professional
priority. Training in Officer Candidate School gal-
vanized that commitment. His loyal, dedicated service was second to none.

Phyllis was very much in love with Richard,
but his injury changed him. He lost his ability to
recall people and events. Trying with all her might
to reconnect with him after his memory loss, she

became understandably frustrated. She accepted that through no fault of his own he was a changed man and the chances of returning to his old self were slim and none. Phyllis and Richard's therapist tried unsuccessfully to normalize him but overcoming the scientific reality of his injury was simply not feasible. His brain impairment was unalterable. Accordingly, after much personal consternation, Phyllis decided to separate from Richard, choosing to move in a new and positive direction with her life. As the saying goes, Life can be understood backwards; but it must be lived forward.

EPILOGUE
(7 YEARS LATER)

The cemetery on the outskirts of town commemorated local war veterans with a unique edifice honoring their service and sacrifice. Each deceased soldier, seaman, and airman bore an inscription on their bronze marker. Richard was among them. Dead from a cancerous brain tumor, Phyllis visited him once a year on his birthday. Married to Lawrence, she was now Phyllis Andersen. They were blessed with two adorable children — a boy, David four years old and a girl, Sarah, three. Lawrence was promoted several times at his company and continued to play the piano just for fun.

He particularly enjoyed playing at his children's birthday parties. Essentially a stay-at-home mom, Phyllis worked part time, mainly weekends, at a new medical clinic in Elbow Lake. She remained devoted to nursing and enjoyed the interaction with staff and patients. Her dream of a loving husband, nice home, raising a family, and happiness was finally a reality, and she was very grateful.

Richard's death broke his mother's spirit and she succumbed after suffering a massive heart attack. Ben James, dejected and alone, lost his family. Seeing him somber at work more often than not, a customer gifted him a yellow English Labrador puppy. Feisty and adorable, the dog who Ben named Jasper gave Ben unconditional love, something he didn't experience in his marriage. His wish to have grandchildren never materialized but, thankfully, Phyllis and Lawrence 's children adopted him. Often invited over for Sunday dinner, he became an "honorary" grandfather - "Popo," as David and Sarah called him. He babysat them whenever asked. Michael and Cheryl Verducci were slowing down a bit, but they dedicated time, energy, and spared no expense doting over their grandchildren. Spoiling them was their favorite pastime.

Ellen matriculated to the same college in North Dakota where Phyllis attended and earned a degree in teaching. Upon graduation she was hired to teach fourth grade at an elementary school in Elbow Lake. She and Phyllis remained great friends and, as expected, Ellen performed duties as another willing and able babysitter for David and Sarah. Periodically, Phyllis and Ellen enjoyed a girls' night out. On one occasion, Phyllis admitted she missed Richard and fondly recalled some of their great times together. Citing the awful war, she said his death was tragic but, in some way, or another, his dedicated service helped win the war. Known only to her, she placed his two Purple Hearts and the Distinguished Service Cross in a special locked box in her dresser. On top was his letter, still unopened, and wrapped in tissue the diamond wedding ring he bestowed on her thirteen years earlier. In her mind and heart, Richard would always be her hero.

ABOUT THE AUTHOR

 Rich has authored seven published works including *Classroom Under Construction, Angel in my Backpack, Old - Stories of Aging and Reflections on Caregiving, Cat Speak*, and two children's books, *Animal Friends* and *Heather and Buddy Go to School*. Rich's writing reflects his interest in diverse topics, both fiction and nonfiction, based on his educational and professional background, affinity for the imagination and wonder of children, respect for aging, interest in the history of global conflicts, and his own creative instincts.

Two more children's books are in the works to complete the *Heather and Buddy* trilogy. *Heather and Buddy Go to the Zoo* is next - due for publication later this year. High school coach, principal mentor, writing workshop presenter, hospice volunteer, and storyteller, Rich is blessed with two beautiful, grown daughters and four adorable grandchildren.

He lives in Ventura, California.

www.richgrimesbooks.com

www.ingramcontent.com/pod-product-compliance
Lightning Source LLC
Chambersburg PA
CBHW051251250626
47155CB00009B/3260